his outback temptation

a Pickle Creek novel

his outback temptation

a Pickle Creek novel

ANNIE SEATON

Entangled Publishing, LLC
2614 South Timberline Road
Suite 105, PMB 159
Fort Collins, CO 80525
rights@entangledpublishing.com

Bliss is an imprint of Entangled Publishing, LLC.

Edited by Erin Molta
Cover design by April Martinez
Cover photography from iStock and Shutterstock

Manufactured in the United States of America

First Edition May 2018

To my three gorgeous grandchildren: Benny, Charlotte, and Charlie.
Follow your dreams.

Glossary of Aussie terms

Billy: a tin with a lid and a wire handle used for boiling water, making tea, etc. over an open fire.

Bore: a bore is where you find groundwater that has been accessed by drilling into underground water storages called aquifers.

CWA: (Country Women's Association) The CWA is the largest women's organisation in Australia and aims to improve conditions for country women and children.

Dam: a reservoir used as a water supply.

Esky: a portable insulated container for keeping food or drink cool.

Fair dinkum: fair or true

Farm stay: paid accommodation on a farm

Flat chat: at full speed, going as fast as you possibly can.

Jack Robinson: fast or quick

Jaffle Iron: a device for making toasted sandwiches over an open fire, consisting of two hinged metal plates on a long handle.

Milk bar: a corner shop that sells milkshakes and other refreshments.

Paddock: small field

Pajero: A type of four-wheel drive vehicle.

Pikelets: a thin kind of crumpet

Prickle: a short, pointed outgrowth on a plant; a small thorn.

Pilliga Scrub: is a forest of some 3,000 km2 of semi-arid woodland in temperate north-central New South Wales, Australia.

Rissole: A slang abbreviation for RSL.

Rouseabout: an unskilled labourer or odd jobber on a farm, especially in a shearing shed.

RSL: The Returned and Services League, Australia (RSL) is a support organisation for men and women who have served or are serving in the Defence Force and provides a social club in communities.

Smoko: a rest from work for a tea or coffee break.

Swag: In Australia, a "swag" is a portable "sleeping unit." A small tent with a mattress included made from heavy duty canvas.

Ute: a utility vehicle; a pickup in Australia or New Zealand.

Prologue

Two years earlier

Sebastian Richards put down his camera and pulled the buzzing phone from his pocket. "You can take a break, kids." He forced a smile to his face as he gestured to the mother of the small children he was shooting for the department store catalogue. The little boy poked his tongue at Sebastian as he ran past, and he thanked his lucky stars for the call that had interrupted the photo shoot from hell. The little fiend's sister aimed a kick at Seb's ankles and stood there and stared at him.

God, I love kids, but I sure hate working with them.

He was so preoccupied watching for the kicking feet of the child from hell, he didn't look at the screen before he pressed answer. "Seb Richards."

His blood ran cold as he listened to the voice on the other end.

The last person he expected to call him. He turned away from the small girl, not caring if he got kicked to kingdom come. It would be preferable to talking to his grandmother.

"Sebastian."

"Hello, Gran."

"I want you all to come home."

"All who?"

"Don't be smart, boy. You and your cousins."

"Sorry, Gran. I'm at work. I'll call you back." He disconnected before she could reply and shoved the phone back into his pocket.

"Sorry, Mrs Armitage. That was…er, business. I have to go. Take your kids out for some lunch, and we'll meet back here at two o'clock."

He grabbed his camera and tripod and ran down the stairs. If he was quick he could get to the office on the next floor before the old bat called Lucy.

But he was too late. Gran had already rung not only Lucy but their other two cousins, as well.

Lucy stared at him, her brow wrinkled and her eyes full of worry. "Do you want to travel back with me?"

"What? Back to the Pilliga Scrub? Come on, Lucy, you're not seriously considering going home?"

No, not home. It wasn't home. And it hadn't been for a long time.

He shook his head. In the old days when they'd all lived in the small country town of Spring Downs—family holidays, Christmas, and many a weekend had been spent out of town at Gran and Pop's farm. The whole family would pack up and head to the farm—the three sisters and his three cousins—but it wasn't home anymore.

"You're not really going back to Spring Downs, are you?" he asked.

"Yes, and you have to come. Gran said Jemmy and Liam have already agreed."

Sebastian's eyes were wide. "What? You mean Mr.-High-Achiever-the-world-famous-journalist, is coming home from

London? No way! Not only will I come up and see that but I'll eat my hat and run around the paddock stark bollocky naked if Liam comes home."

"I'll hold you to that," she said quietly. "Gran was sure he was coming. So now the three of us have said yes, and if you agree that'll make all four of us."

"Damnation, bloody hell, and bollocks." Sebastian's voice was cross, but he couldn't help it. "I don't want to."

"You sound like the whining six-year-old you used to be." Lucy reached out and touched his arm. "Come on, Seb. I don't think Gran's real well. But she won't say what's wrong unless we're all there. So get yourself on your bike and get out there."

"All right. I know I'm being difficult, but damn it, I'd rather step into a nest of vipers than in front the old bat."

"I honestly don't know what's got into you, Seb. Gran is a sweetheart."

"All right, all right. I said I'll go out there. But I won't be staying."

Chapter One

The present

Sebastian leaned his head back on the soft black leather headrest and closed his eyes. The comforting drone of the engines soothed the strange restlessness that had filled him ever since he'd boarded the plane in Rome. Choosing to travel business class from Europe might have been an extravagance, but hey, he'd worked hard for the past two years. His destination was a long way from the luxury apartment he'd shared in Florence. Spending some of his savings on making the long flight back to Sydney more comfortable had been a no-brainer. If he had to spend time back at the farm, he would have a comfortable trip getting there.

How long would he be there?

A few months?

A few years?

Sebastian still hadn't got his head around the fact that he was going home.

A long while.

The rest of my life?

Spring Downs was good enough for his cousins, and now it was time for him to do the right thing by his family. Since Gran had called them all home two years back, Lucy, Liam, and Jemima had taken their turns and gone home to Spring Downs to look after their grandparents' farm. One by one they'd decided to settle in the Pilliga Scrub where they'd grown up. And when he'd come home to the Outback for a visit—not that it had been very often—their contentment had surprised him.

Maybe he was even a little bit jealous. If the truth be known, watching the three people he was closest to fall in love and settle happily with their respective partners had left him a little bit hollow and lonely. And that was way out of character for him

"Love-'em-and-leave-'em Seb" was the nickname given to him by his colleagues in the business. Somehow, Liam had gotten wind of that nickname back home, probably from Lucy when Seb and Lucy had worked together at the advertising agency in Sydney. Of course, it had gone through the family, and Gran had shaken her head and tutted about it when he'd visited.

So he had a reputation as a bit of a playboy. Let them think what they liked. He enjoyed life, and he knew he could make a go of whatever the Outback threw at him.

But he hadn't gone home very often. He knew he was a disappointment to his family but that was their problem, not his. Gran kept going on about how *lucky* he was.

What a great life Seb has.

"Sebastian has an easy job," she told everyone. Clicking away and taking photos was a breeze compared to the hot dry work in the paddocks at Prickle Creek Farm. "He is so lucky," Gran would say, "not to mention they pay him a ridiculous amount of money to swan around the world."

Well, it was time to come home and prove that he could work as hard as the rest of the family.

Sebastian shook his head and reached for the glass of fizzy water that the air steward placed on the tray beside him. Whoever would have thought that a graphic designer, a journalist, and an international supermodel would be happy and settled in a small farming region on the edge of the Outback? Now a freelance photographer would be joining them.

It was time to see what coming home to Spring Downs would do for him.

No one knew the grief he'd carried inside since his mother had been killed in a car accident. No one knew how much he longed for the vast open plains of the Pilliga Scrub... sometimes.

Maybe it *was* time to settle down to real work. A bitter smile tugged at Sebastian's lips.

Gran's words, not mine.

• • •

Isabella Romano caught the eye of the female steward as she walked up the aisle towards the service area at the back of the economy section. "Excuse me? May I have some more water please?"

"I'll be back in a moment," the steward replied with a smile.

As Isabella waited, she took the opportunity to move farther to the right. Closer to the armrest of the aisle seat, and as far away as she could get from her fellow passenger. Ever since she'd reboarded the plane after the brief refueling stopover in Singapore, the guy sitting beside her had talked nonstop. Even putting the earphones in and trying to watch a movie hadn't worked. Whenever she tried looking at the screen, he'd touch her wrist to get her attention back. He was driving her crazy.

Harmless but a pain in the arse.

She'd heard all about his trip to China. How much he'd hated the food. How he'd hated the crowds. And then he'd started on how much he'd hated his job and wasn't looking forward to going home. He leaned closer and the stale smell of his clothes almost made her gag. She bit her lip as his long, greasy hair brushed her shoulder when he settled in his seat.

"And my boss sucks, too," he added.

"Maybe you could take another vacation," Isabella had said politely, inching as far towards the aisle as she could.

And then he'd started on about how he'd used all his leave up and couldn't afford it, anyway.

She deserved a medal. Four hours into the flight and he hadn't shut up for one minute.

Four hours down, three hours and twelve minutes to go.

"Thank you." Isabella took the plastic cup from the steward and sipped at it. She tried to ignore the conversation coming from her left. Sadly, she'd already sussed out the plane, and there wasn't a spare seat to be had.

"So tell me all about yourself. I think we're going to be friends," the creepy guy said. "I still don't even know your name. Let's go out for a drink tonight in Sydney."

What?

The hide of him! For all he knew she could be catching a connecting flight as soon as they landed. She considered using that as an excuse, and then she straightened in her seat and gave him a cool look.

"I'm not staying long enough in Australia to become friends with anyone."

God, I'm an idiot. Don't engage in conversation. Don't tell him anything.

Why do I find it so hard to be rude to anyone? This guy was certainly overstepping the boundaries of polite behaviour, and he didn't deserve a response at all, let alone a polite one.

But of course he pounced on her words, and she spent the next three hours avoiding even more personal questions.

Eventually, he began to really creep her out.

As they prepared for landing, he pulled out a pen and scrawled his number on the back of the napkin that he'd already wiped across his mouth.

Ugh.

If they hadn't been so close to landing, she would have begged the steward to find her another seat, even though she'd walked the length of the plane a couple more times and it was full.

Finally, the FASTEN SEAT BELT light stayed on, and those wonderful words, "prepare the cabin for landing" came over the loudspeaker.

Chapter Two

"Sebastian!"

Seb turned around as he heard his name over the hubbub of noise in the queue to passport control. Before he could blink, a small body slammed into his. All he got was a fleeting look at wide dark eyes, lush red lips, and a tangle of black curly hair before a pair of arms wound tightly around his neck.

"Kiss me, quick. Please help me," a husky voice demanded a second before warm, soft lips pressed against his. "As if you can't bear to let me go."

Who am I to argue with such a request? The voice and the quick glimpse of the face were familiar. It was someone he knew, and as he returned the kiss, he tried to remember where he'd seen her pretty face before.

In a bar in Sydney? At the office?

Without breaking the lip-lock, he managed to slide his camera bag down beside his feet. The mystery woman bent with him as he leaned, and the firm arms didn't leave his neck when he straightened again.

"Don't stop. Please." Those soft lips were warm and welcoming as she pressed her mouth even more firmly against his. "Keep kissing me." All at once Sebastian realised that the woman's voice was shaking and surprise jolted through him. Whoever she was, she wasn't crazy, or playing games; she was plain scared. A sweet, lemony fragrance surrounded him as he put his arms around a tiny waist. His hands brushed against some sort of silky material, but he could still feel the soft curves beneath it. Sebastian couldn't help the smile that tipped his lips. He went to pull back to look at her to see who he was actually kissing.

"No, no. Don't stop yet." The lilt of her accent was tugging at his memory. Someone from Italy?

"Okay. It might be a moot point, but at least tell me who I'm kissing." His words were muffled against her lips.

He felt her lips lift in a smile against his. His nerve endings tingled as she lifted her hands and wound her fingers in his hair to hold his head firmly against hers. Not that he wanted to go anywhere.

"Bella."

Closing his eyes, he tried to remember a Bella from his past. "Bella who?"

"Lucy's friend. Isabella from Spring Downs High School."

"Bella? Isabella Romano?" Sebastian frowned as the lips vibrated against his. He'd never had such a long conversation during a kiss before.

"Yes."

She tasted minty and fresh.

It must have been at least ten years since he'd last seen Bella. He and Lucy had been in high school when she'd moved to Spring Downs. Lucy had held down a part-time job for one summer at the milk bar that Isabella's father owned. *Con's Milk Bar.* He'd never found a milkshake that tasted as good as Con's.

"Come on, mate. You're holding up the queue." The impatient demand came from behind them. Sebastian lifted his head a fraction and looked ahead to the electronic passport control booth. He had been so absorbed in the unexpected kiss, he hadn't noticed the queue move forward, and now there was a huge gap between them and the person about to step into the booth. It was their turn next.

The short, fat guy with long, greasy hair standing behind them glared at him.

"Please don't stop," Isabella whispered, pulling his head down again. "Make it look as though you've missed me. Really, really missed me."

She was crazy.

"Sorry, sweetheart. It's our turn to go through passport control. You'll have to let me go," Sebastian said, his lips still against hers.

"Can you keep your arm around me, and then let me go first? I'll wait for you at the other side?" He obliged, lifting his arm and putting it around her shoulders and holding her close as he reached down for his camera bag.

"Wait for me there. I missed you, darling," he said loudly. Lowering his head he pretended to brush her cute little ear with his lips but he whispered, "It's okay. I get it now. Don't worry."

The guy behind them reached over and tapped Isabella's arm as Sebastian hefted the camera bag onto his shoulder. "You forgot to take the napkin," he said in a whiny voice, shoving a stained paper napkin at Isabella.

"No, thank you." She lifted her head briefly from where she'd snuggled into Sebastian's shoulder. Sebastian didn't recall that she'd had an accent when they'd been at high school, although she hadn't been in Spring Downs for long before she'd left again. Not that he'd spent much time with

Isabella back then. She'd just been one of the girls at school. He stared down at her as she lifted her chin and turned away from the man behind them.

"And I missed you too, Seb."

"If you missed each other so much, why weren't you sitting together?" The guy was persistent and Sebastian narrowed his eyes.

As he crowded their space, Isabella moved closer to Sebastian—if it were possible. Most of her body was already stuck to his like a limpet.

The guy's tone was full of belligerence. "I said, 'Why weren't you sitting with him on the plane?'"

Sebastian lowered his head and brushed his lips against Isabella's ear. "Do you know this guy, Bella?"

The shake of her head was almost imperceptible.

"I don't think that's any of your business, mate." While his words were firm, Sebastian kept his smile friendly. "But for your information, I was upgraded to business class, and I wasn't able to sit with my *fiancée*."

The passport control booth lit up and, turning his back, he blocked the guy's view of Isabella as she hurried forward with her passport open ready to scan. When she was through he followed quickly, placed his passport on the scanner, and as soon as the green light flashed he hurried after her. He walked beside her as she rushed through the "nothing to declare" entry to customs.

"I'll come to the baggage carousel with you," he said. "I don't like that guy's attitude."

"Me neither, and thanks. I really appreciate that," she said, flicking a nervous glance over her shoulder. "Once we get our bags I'll explain why I threw myself at you. You would not believe how relieved I was to see someone I knew." For the first time, a glimmer of humour was in Isabella's voice.

"My pleasure. Happy to oblige."

The slight flush that stained her cheeks made her even prettier. Sebastian stayed with Isabella while she retrieved her small bag, and then she stood beside him while he went over to the special luggage section to arrange for the delivery of his photographic equipment to Spring Downs. The nuisance guy seemed to have disappeared, but Sebastian wasn't going to risk leaving her alone. If the guy came back and bothered her again, he'd call airport security.

"So what now?" Sebastian swung his travel pack onto his back and reached down for Isabella's bag. "Do you want to share a taxi?"

Isabella bit her lips as he watched. "Are you staying in the city?" she asked.

"No. I'm collecting my motorbike from a storage unit at Botany, and then I'm heading out to Spring Downs later today. What about you?"

"Um." That lip biting thing she did was really cute. He couldn't take his eyes from her mouth; her lips were rosy and full.

And kissable. He could vouch for that firsthand. Another warm tingle ran through him and he smiled at her.

"Well, would you believe I'm going to Spring Downs, too?" she said, and that gorgeous mouth opened into a smile, revealing a row of perfect white teeth.

"Fair dinkum! That's a happy coincidence. I thought you moved away when we were in high school?"

"I did. Mum and I moved back to Italy, but—"

Sebastian put a hand on her arm. "Look, I'm starving. How about a coffee before we head out into the peak-hour rush? It'll be a better place for catching up than standing around in the airport."

He grinned when she nodded.

• • •

Isabella had been so relieved to recognise Sebastian at the airport she hadn't entertained a second thought when she'd hurried over to him and demanded a kiss. Convincing that sleazy guy that she was with someone had been uppermost in her mind. It had been dicey for a while when he'd insisted on knowing why they hadn't been sitting together, but Sebastian had picked up on the situation quickly and handled it adroitly.

What a jerk that guy had been.

She waited at the table Sebastian had snagged while he went over to order their coffee.

"Short black, please. Double shot," she'd answered when he asked her what she'd like. "I need to wake up a bit and get myself organised."

While Sebastian stood at the counter Isabella checked him out.

He sure could kiss. That's one thing she'd discovered about the grown-up Sebastian. He'd been tall at high school, but he'd grown even more, both in height and width. A tight black T-shirt moulded his broad chest, and his narrow black jeans hugged powerful thighs. His hair was pulled back from his face with a leather tie into a short tail. He looked more suited to the city than Spring Downs, with his movie star good looks. As tall and broad as those Hemsworth brothers who were in the magazine she'd tried to read on the flight.

She wondered if he lived there or if he was just visiting.

Sebastian was probably visiting like she was. He looked way too sophisticated to be living out in the boondocks. As he turned, she looked down, pretending to fiddle with her phone, not wanting to be caught blatantly checking him out.

"One short black, double shot." He put the coffee down in front of her and pulled out the chair opposite her.

"Where's yours?" she asked with a frown.

"They'll call me over when it's ready. I'm having a chocolate milkshake. It's the one thing I've craved while I've been in Italy."

Isabella smiled and picked up the packet of sugar to tip into her coffee. "Have you been over there on holidays?"

"No, I was working." Sebastian leaned back in the chair, and for the first time she noticed a small diamond glinting in his earlobe.

Very cosmopolitan.

"Now tell me about that guy who was hassling you." He leaned forward with a frown.

"It was nothing major. I was probably overreacting. He was in the seat next to me all the way from Singapore, and he was very persistent. He just wouldn't stop talking."

"You should have called the steward."

"No." She shook her head. "There was nothing to report. He was just persistent and a little bit sleazy. He didn't do or say anything bad. I got off the plane as quick as I could, but then he was right behind me. I panicked when he tried to hold my arm. And then, I saw you, just at the right time." She picked up the spoon and stirred her coffee. "Like I said, I was overreacting. But I didn't feel comfortable going to sleep with him beside me so I'm extra tired now."

"What about you? Were you on holiday over there?" he asked, and she was pleased at the subject change. Enough of Mr. Creepy Guy.

"No. I was working, too. Where were you working?" she asked.

Sebastian waited until the waitress from the coffee shop put his milkshake in front of him. "Thank you. I could have come and collected it." His smile lit up the room, and the waitress lingered for a moment smiling back.

Isabella bit back her own smile.

Sebastian oozed charm. Bucket loads. But in a nice way.

She remembered his family from school. There were a few of them, and they'd been a very tight bunch. There'd been

some tragedy with a road accident about the time she and
Mum had left town, but she couldn't remember exactly what
it was.

She pushed away the sad sigh that hovered.

Poor Dad. He's been all alone there a long time.

"I'm a photographer and I had a few contracts with a
couple of Italian companies," he said.

"Rome?" She tilted her head to the side. "Or fashion in
Milan?"

"No, tourism in Florence. What about you?"

"Wow! Really?" She stared at him. "What a coincidence!
I've been in Florence for the past eight years. Ever since Mum
and I left Spring Downs." Her voice was quiet. "Dad stayed.
He's doing it a bit tough at the moment. That's why I'm going
for a visit."

"What a shame we didn't hook up in Florence. You could
have shown me the sights."

"I'm sure if you were a tourist photographer you saw
most of them."

Sebastian picked up his milkshake, and Isabella smiled
at the look of bliss that crossed his face as he drank it. "Yum.
That is so good." He wiped his hand over his mouth when he
came up for breath.

"Looks like you're enjoying that." She shook her head.
His appearance was more suited to someone drinking a
trendy coffee, not slurping a milkshake like a schoolboy.
"Where did you live?"

"Just off Santo Spirito *Piazza.*" He drained the last of
his drink and then dipped the straw in the froth and licked
it. Isabella giggled. It *was* just like being back in high school
again in Dad's milk bar after school. It had been a long time
since she'd sat beside a boy—no, a man, a gorgeous man—
drinking a milkshake. Usually, it was some chef trying to
entice her into a fancy cocktail after a busy night in a hot

kitchen.

"You?" he asked.

"I'm not making this up." She put her elbow on the table and propped her chin in her hand. "But would you believe not far from Santo Spirito? Closer to the Pitti Palace end, near the Boboli Gardens."

"Small world. I walked down there most mornings." He shook his head and reached back to tie the leather when it slipped off his ponytail. "So tell me about your trip home to Spring Downs. Your dad is still there, you said?"

"Yes, he still owns the local milk bar. I'll have to get you a friend's discount."

"Your dad is Con, isn't he? Lucy worked there one summer."

"He *is* Con the Greek." She giggled. "But he's actually Italian, and his name is Leonardo."

Sebastian's brow wrinkled in a frown, but he smiled and Isabella caught her breath. He was such a great-looking guy, and when he smiled at you—like he had at the waitress a minute ago—he seemed to focus exclusively on you and blocked out everything else. Like you were the only thing in his world at that exact moment. She sat up straight and shook her head again.

Charm unlimited. He was hard to resist.

"When Dad took over Con's Milk Bar, everyone called him Con, so he answered to it."

"Love it. I'll make sure I call in for a milkshake. But I don't expect mate's rates."

"So tell me about you coming back to Spring Downs," she said. "A quick visit like mine? Family duty and all that?"

"No, to a quick visit, but yes to the family duty bit. I'm going home to stay."

"That's a big change from Italy. What are you going to do? There's not a lot of work for a photographer in Spring

Downs, is there?"

"My grandparents have retired, and my cousins have taken over the Prickle Creek Farm. Well, mainly Liam, now that Lucy's married and lives on another farm. I was supposed to be there ages ago, but I couldn't knock the Italian contract back."

"Lucy's married? Wow, it seems like no time at all since I was friends with Lucy and Jemmy at high school. So once you arrive, the old gang will be back together."

"Yep. But they've all settled down. They fell back in love with the place and found 'love.'"

"You sound cynical." Isabella drained her coffee and put the cup back onto the saucer.

"It's all been a bit quick for me. One minute they were each immersed in a career, and then we got called home, and before you could say 'Jack Robinson' all three of them were getting married."

Isabella shrugged. "Cupid's arrow. It's a bit like that."

"You sound like you speak from experience."

"Oh *Dio,* no. I'm too busy working to fall in love with anyone."

"What do you do?"

"I'm a chef." Excitement flooded through her. "After I visit Dad, I'm going to England. I'm starting a job in one of the *best* restaurants over there."

"Congratulations. I love the UK. I flew over for a few weekends when I was in Italy." Sebastian glanced at his watch. "Okay, I'd better get going. So how are you getting to Spring Downs?"

"I'm not sure yet." Isabella shrugged. "Dad got his dates mixed up when I first told him I was coming to visit. Would you believe he drove all the way to Sydney and turned up at the airport to collect me six months ago! I said September and he swore I wrote February in the email. He is such a ditz sometimes. So I didn't tell him I was coming today. I said I'd make my own way there. I'll have to catch a coach to Narrabri or Dubbo and maybe hire a car."

Sebastian glanced down at her small bag. "You travel light. Would you like a lift? Or should I say a ride?"

She thought for a brief second and then nodded. "Thank you. That would be great!"

Chapter Three

Three hours later, Sebastian was on his BMW. The thrill of the speed and the wind whistling past his face—not to mention the woman sitting behind him with her hands resting lightly on his waist—had soothed his mood. He wouldn't admit it to his cousins—or Gran—but he was hesitant about going back to the farm. But he had something to prove, not only to the family, but to himself as well.

His trepidation dissipated as the powerful bike flew along the highway. Sebastian had missed the bush. There was nothing like the colours of the paddocks and the big open sky out west. Even the thought of the red dust and the prickles of the Pilliga Scrub enticed him. The paddocks were full of fat cattle, and the grass along the edge of the road was lush and green for a change. Liam had said they'd had a lot of winter rain, and the glossy coats of the cattle showed how good the season had been.

He grinned beneath his helmet as he leaned into a sweeping curve north of Dunedoo.

Still a country boy, checking out the cattle.

Isabella leaned with him and held on tight. She whooped behind him. It hadn't taken much to get her sorted for the ride home. He had a spare helmet and leathers in the unit where the bike was stored, and it had taken less than an hour to get them both kitted up and on the highway.

As he slowed for some cattle crossing the road just before Dubbo, he turned to her. "Happy to take another quick break?"

"Sounds good. I have a numb bum." Her chuckle surrounded him and he smiled as the cattle ambled into the paddock, and the bike surged forwards. The small city of Dubbo wasn't far ahead. "But this is great. I'd forgotten how beautiful the Australian bush is."

Isabella had been the ideal pillion passenger. Not one complaint, and apart from an earlier quick stop, they'd been on the bike continuously for just under five hours. After this break they had less than two hours to go before they reached Spring Downs. He'd be sorry to drop her off, but he'd definitely see her again once he got settled.

Even though it sounds like she's only here for a short visit.

Sebastian turned the bike into the large highway service centre just north of Dubbo on the Castlereagh Highway. Isabella unclipped the helmet, removed it, and as she shook her head her black curls tumbled onto her shoulders. Sebastian stared as she combed her fingers through her hair with a laugh.

"I need coffee, please. I was getting sleepy before you stopped for those cattle." Her smile was wide and, once again, he was struck by her beauty. He didn't remember noticing that at high school, but in those days, he'd probably been more interested in motorbikes than pretty girls. She reminded him of that character in the fairy tale.

The one with the red lips, fair skin, and black hair. Rose Red?

"What's wrong? Have I got smut on my face?" Those pretty teeth flashed in another smile.

Seb was jerked out of his daydreaming. "No, no. You're fine. I was miles away."

Her look was curious. "I know you said you're here to stay, but how do you like the idea of coming back to the Pilliga after two years in Florence?"

"Why do you ask?" he said carefully.

"I couldn't live here. There's nothing here for me." Isabella peeled off the leather jacket and put it on the back of the bike. "But each to his own. Lead on, Sebastian. Coffee calls."

"I need food." As he followed her to the café, he mulled over her words.

Sebastian had loved being at the farm when he was a teenager, but in Gran's eyes nothing he did had ever measured up to Liam, his oldest cousin. So he'd turned himself into a city boy. In his signature black turtlenecks, black jeans, and his long ponytail, he'd roamed the bars with his camera, snapping the in-crowd for the social pages and doing department store catalogues until Lucy had gotten him a start at the agency where she worked. His career had skyrocketed, and the past two years in Europe had put him at the top of his field. To his colleagues, Sebastian was the consummate metro-sexual of the trendy crowd. No one realised a country boy still lurked beneath his city exterior.

There *was* something for him here. Family. And Prickle Creek Farm.

There was.

It would be enough.

It would.

• • •

Sebastian was quiet as they sat waiting for their meal and Isabella worried that she'd upset him. She racked her brains for a clue, but they hadn't spoken much since they'd ordered. Maybe he was regretting offering her the ride.

"Are you stopping in Spring Downs or is your farm this side of town? Would it be easier if I called my dad and got him to meet us out on the highway?"

"No, it's fine. Our farm's way out on the other side of town, and besides, I need to get my payment from you for the ride out."

"Oh, okay." Isabella was happy to throw in cash for the trip, but she was surprised at him calling it "payment." "Of course. I'll throw in for the fuel."

Sebastian shook his head. "No, no, I was coming this way anyway. All I want is a famous Con's Milk Bar milkshake. With malt. Those malted milkshakes make up some of my best memories of growing up in town."

Isabella laughed. "For sure. Not a problem."

They sat quietly as their late lunch was delivered. She picked at her salad as Sebastian devoured a huge steak sandwich and chips.

"Not up to your chef standards?" He glanced at her barely touched food as he wiped his mouth with his napkin. It was prepackaged, and she wasn't really hungry.

But she felt as though she was being judged and a little niggle of anger settled in her chest.

"No. It's fine." She knew her voice was clipped, but she hated being criticised. "Jet lag affects my appetite. I'm not a foodie snob."

"I wasn't suggesting you were." His brow creased in a slight frown, and he looked uncomfortable. "Sorry, I didn't mean to sound critical."

She waved her hand. "No, I'm sorry for snapping. Just another side effect of jet lag. And I guess, if I'm honest, I'm really not looking forward to the next six weeks." She rushed on when he raised his eyebrows and a flicker of interest sparked inside her as he held her gaze. He really was a good-looking guy. Maybe she'd see him around town while she was here. "I mean, it'll be great to see Dad and sort him out, but how the heck am I going to fill in time in Spring Downs? I've lost touch with anyone I knew back in high school. But I will call Lucy, for sure."

He nodded. "I guess it's going to be a bit of a cultural shock for you. No theatres, no coffee shops, no galleries, nothing like what you're used to in Florence."

"I know. At least I'll have a good rest while I'm here. I've been working long hours in a restaurant in Florence. I can catch up on lots of reading. And try out some new recipe ideas I have ready for my new job."

"I could provide you with some social life." His face lit up in a wide grin.

She tipped her head to the side and smiled back. "You can?"

"You can come out to the farm and catch up with Lucy and Jemmy. And meet Angie, too. She lived in London with Liam."

"That would be nice. I'll look forward to it." An unfamiliar shyness ran through her, so with a forced chuckle she changed the subject. "I do have one goal for when I'm here. I'm going to convince Dad that he has to go back to Italy and visit Mum. Maybe even stay there."

"That's what you meant by sorting him out before?" Sebastian held her eyes, and his voice was full of sympathy.

"Yes. Mum went back to Italy to 'find' herself. They're both so damn stubborn, neither will give in. Dad won't move back to Italy because he's trying to prove to Mum that he's the boss, and she won't live over here. So both of them have settled for second best over the past few years just to prove a point."

"So what's your plan?"

"I don't have one yet. All it would take to get them back together would be for Dad to follow Mum, and they'd sort it out." Isabella leaned back and crossed her arms. "But unfortunately, or fortunately, for both of them, depends which way they take it, I'm determined. If I have a goal, I achieve it. No matter *what* it takes."

"And I guess that's how you got this fabulous job in England."

She nodded. "It's been my dream for the last five years. I'm so excited about it. The restaurant is in a little village near Windsor and it's called The Three Ducks. The owner is one of those celebrity chefs, and it's one of the top four restaurants in England. Very sought-after place to work."

"And you snagged a job there." Sebastian held out his hand. "Well done."

"Not so much snagged as put in a lot of hard work to get it." His fingers were warm against hers.

"You'll get on very well with Liam."

"Liam?"

"My cousin. The oldest of the four of us. He's got a work ethic like you wouldn't believe, and he's always trying to—" Sebastian broke off, pulled his hand back, and glanced at his watch. "Enough of that. Come on, let's hit the road."

Isabella wondered what he was going to say and what Liam was always trying to do.

She shrugged. It wasn't her business.

Chapter Four

As Sebastian rode down the main street of Spring Downs after dropping Isabella at Con's Milk Bar, he tried to summon up some excitement about going to Prickle Creek Farm. He was here to stay, so he'd better get the enthusiasm fired up. He was committed to seeing this through, even though it was going to be a big change for him. Once he was back on the farm this unsettled feeling would go away. The uncertainty of whether he'd made the right choice would disappear once he got to work.

It was probably jet lag, on top of the hard work he'd put in over the past few months to complete the contracted work in Italy, but the only excitement he was feeling at the moment was thinking about Isabella's lips on his at the airport. He'd made sure that he got her mobile number, and he'd promised a catch up in the next few days.

"Before the boredom takes hold," he'd whispered as she'd handed the spare helmet to him. Her father had shaken his hand and welcomed him back to town. Sebastian had declined the milkshake that Isabella had offered.

"No, but thanks, I'm still full from that burger. And Liam will have a cold beer waiting to celebrate the return of the prodigal cousin." He'd leaned over and kissed Isabella's cheeks, European style, and she'd smiled back at him. "Thanks for the company."

"Thanks for the lift. You saved me heaps of time," she'd said.

"More time to spend in Spring Downs, hey?"

They'd shared a look and her smile had widened. He'd be coming back to town sooner rather than later to catch up.

The BMW chewed up the narrow highway out to the farm turn-off. One consolation, Gran and Pop were still away. They'd been travelling around the world for the past two years but were due home for the double family wedding that was taking place in a month. He and Gran had never seen eye to eye. She seemed to always pick on him. Luckily, he'd learned to cope with that, just as he'd learned to deal with difficult bosses.

It wasn't his fault that everything he wanted came to him easily. Liam, Lucy, and Jemima knew he hated the "Lucky" nickname, so of course they'd teased him mercilessly until he'd lost his temper one day and had dunked Liam in the bore.

The nickname had been long forgotten. He hoped.

Put away along with many other emotions. The grief that had consumed them all when Gran and Pop's three daughters had been killed in that car accident had eased over the years.

Never forgotten, always there, but more bearable as time had passed. Lucy's mum, Liam and Jemima's mum, and his own beautiful mother had never returned from the trip they'd taken together—one they'd talked about for such a long time. His mum had been a single mother. His father had walked away when she'd announced she was pregnant with Sebastian, and he'd never been a part of his life.

Lucky? Sebastian didn't think so.

Anyway, now he was back home, back where he'd grown up and had a happy childhood. He'd seen the world and worked in the cities. It was time to settle down and show Liam—and Gran—that he was capable of working just as hard as anyone to run the farm.

Sebastian slowed the bike as he approached the cattle grid at the front gate. His eyes widened as he read the new sign at the gate:

PRICKLE CREEK FARM

OWNERS: L. SMYTHE J.MCCORMACK L.MACKENZIE S. RICHARDS

Bloody hell. Gran and Pop must have signed the farm over to the four of them when they'd been home last time. Liam had said there was news that he'd be surprised to hear but wouldn't tell him what it was until he came home.

He shook his head as he roared up the red dust driveway.

Sebastian Richards, property owner. He would have to make sure he damn well pulled his weight. For the first time a flare of excited anticipation about being home sparked in his gut.

The house yard of Prickle Creek Farm was full of farm utes, Jemmy's silver sports car...and dogs...and kids.

I'm home.

The screen door of the house opened wide, and as he rode the bike into the hayshed, dogs and children trailed behind him. Sebastian smiled at how tidy the shed was. Liam had removed most of the old machinery that Pop had collected over the years. The only piece remaining was the old Massey Ferguson tractor that had belonged to Pop's father.

He climbed off the bike, unclipped his helmet, and as he shed his leather jacket, two young girls ran up to him, closely followed by a small chubby boy.

"Are you Sebastian? Our new mummy's cousin?"

He squatted down onto his haunches and held his hand out. "That would be me."

The little boy looked up at him. "We've seen your photo, but we didn't know you were as tall as Shrek."

"I hope I'm not green like Shrek," he replied with a smile as the little boy took his hand and shook it vigorously.

"I'm Ryan. Daddy taught me how to shake hands. There's nothing worser than a wet fish, you know."

"Hello, Ryan. I'm pleased to meet you and yes, that's true. No wet fish here." Sebastian nodded gravely as he gripped the little boy's hand in a firm clasp. He looked over at the two girls who were standing behind their brother. "Now let me guess. You have to be Kelsey and Gwennie. Which is which?"

The smallest girl stepped forward. "I'm Gwennie."

"I'm Kelsey," the other one said. "And hurry up. We weren't allowed to eat anything before you got here."

"That's because you lot are like a plague of locusts." A familiar voice came from the doorway to the hayshed. "We had to save some food for the guest of honour."

Sebastian stood and held his arms wide open. "Jemmy!"

Jemima stepped in and hugged him. "You look well, Seb."

"And so do you, absolutely glowing." He stepped back and held her at arm's length. Being a mum suits you." He nodded at her pregnant stomach.

"It does." She smiled at the three children standing by them. "And how lucky am I to have three readymade children, too? Now come and see if you remember Ned."

Sebastian pulled the small bag from the back of the bike and slung it over his shoulder.

"Liam and Garth had to go down to the bore to fix one of those motor problems we all seem to have with the pumps out here. I swear it's getting worse. But Lucy and Ned are inside."

"How's the wedding plans going?" he asked as he walked

beside Jemima. He had never seen her so mellow and relaxed.

"Good, but the time is going so fast and there's still a lot to do in the next four weeks."

"Well, I'm home now so an extra pair of hands should lighten the load."

"And you're home to stay, Liam said?" Jemima looked at him curiously.

"Yes, I'm a bit late arriving, but it's my turn to pitch in and do my bit." He frowned. "I noticed the new sign at the gate. Gran and Pop have finally decided to bow out of the farm for good? I haven't talked to them for ages. Gran always says it's too expensive for me to call them all over the world."

"Yes, apparently they started the ball rolling when they were home unexpectedly not long after Lucy had James, but they didn't tell us they'd handed the property over until it was final. Family trusts and companies and old wills slowed it down. Gran said she wrote to you."

"Italian mail is not the most reliable." He grinned. "And God forbid she use email."

"She won't. We still get postcards by snail mail most weeks."

"They'll be home for the wedding, though?"

"They will. But they never tell us when they're coming. They just arrive. Drives Liam crazy."

"Are they going to stay on the farm?" As much as he loved them, Sebastian didn't fancy the idea of sharing a house with his grandparents.

"For the time being, I think they are." Jemima turned as a cloud of red dust appeared to the west. "Here come the men, now. Lucy's in charge of the kitchen, and Ned's out at the barbie. Come and see him before the place turns into a madhouse. You met Angie when you were last home, didn't you?"

"I did."

By the time Liam and Garth had pulled up in the ute, Sebastian had met Ned, hugged Lucy and Angie, cuddled baby James—although he was toddling around now and not so much a baby anymore—and Sebastian had a beer in his hand.

Liam climbed out of the ute and waved to the verandah and then mimicked putting a beer to his mouth. Sebastian waved back, crossed to the beer fridge, and pulled out two more cold bottles.

Garth was first up the steps and shook Sebastian's hand. "Good to see you home again, mate."

Liam walked up slowly and Sebastian noticed his new whipcord toughness. He'd lost weight and hardened up in the two years since he'd taken over the property. He held his hand out, but Liam ignored it and enfolded him in a man hug, thumping his back.

"It's good to have you home, Seb."

Emotion clogged Sebastian's throat. He and Liam had had a difficult relationship after their mothers had died. The teenage years when they'd both been trying to find their place in the pecking order of life had been tough, but they had made their peace in those first couple of weeks when Gran had called them home two years ago, and the four cousins had been at the farm together.

"It's good to be home."

"About bloody time. You can only swan around the world for so long. Now I'm going to put you to real work."

Sebastian brushed the comment off with a laugh and handed Garth and Liam a beer each. They leaned on the railing and looked out over the paddocks.

"The place looks great." Sebastian stared over the waving paddocks of wheat. "Looks like a good harvest is on the way, ready for summer."

"It's been a hard slog to get it this good, but we're on

the home straight now. You were lucky to get that Europe contract when you did. You missed out on the hardest times."

Sebastian bit back the instant retort that sprang to his lips.

Here we go again. *Lucky.*

"I hope you're in good shape, now that you're home to do real work." Liam eyed him over the top of his beer. "Not got soft on all that European food and wine, have you?"

Sebastian tipped the bottle high to take a swig of the icy beer. Look who was talking. Liam had been soft and out of condition when he'd arrived at the farm.

"So a good trip out? Did you come on your bike?" Liam must have noticed he was irritated and changed the subject.

"Yeah. I picked up an unexpected passenger, too. I'll tell you about her over dinner."

Liam shook his head as they walked over to the barbeque together. "You were always good at picking up the ladies." He turned to Ned. "You would have left town by the time Seb grew up, but he was always lucky with the local girls. We all had to struggle to get noticed, but young Seb here used to get the prettiest girls at the dances without even trying, plus he got offered the best part-time jobs in town while we all worked for old Clive at the petrol garage."

"Can't help it if I got all the charm." Sebastian grinned at his cousin.

Ned slapped his thigh. "I'd forgotten about that. I worked for Clive for one whole weekend. He was such a grumpy bugger I went home and told Dad he could pay me for weekend work on the farm."

"Clive's still got the local garage and the repair depot, you know." The conversation turned to local reminiscences and Sebastian stared out over the paddocks. He knew deep down that Liam meant nothing by his ribbing. He was overtired.

"The meat's ready." Ned picked up a tray and slid on the

steaks and the sausages, before topping the meat with the fried onion rings. "Come and eat, everyone."

"Tie the dogs up, Liam, so they don't come around the table." Angie carried a jug of iced water out to the table.

"Not Willow!" Gwennie's voice rose above the barking of the dogs as Liam whistled to them and took them out of the house yard. "Please don't tie Willow up."

"Who's Willow?" Sebastian asked and then chuckled as Liam scooped up a small curly-haired brown spaniel from the lawn.

"Willow is the reason that Angie is marrying me next month. As well as for my awesome cake cooking ability," Liam said, as he ran up the steps with the small dog tucked securely under his arm.

"You believe that, you're in trouble." Angie joined in the lighthearted conversation and Sebastian settled in his chair as Lucy and Jemmy walked out from the kitchen, carrying trays of salads.

"Hang on," he said with a frown. "God, I must be jetlagged because I've just remembered that none of you actually live here anymore. You've all worked hard to get this dinner here tonight, and you brought all this over just because I was arriving?"

"Always quick off the mark is our Seb." Liam shook his head as he sat next to Sebastian and the small dog settled on his lap. "And you're right, wonder boy. Angie and I moved into our new place down by the back bore last month. Jemmy and Ned are across the road at 'Daniela,' and Lucy and Garth are over the back boundary at McKenzie Farm."

"So you won't have to put up with a houseful of kids and dogs when we go home later. You'll have all the peace and quiet you want." Lucy sat on his other side and lifted James onto her lap. "Now tell us about this mystery woman you picked up."

Sebastian laughed. "Gawd, big ears, you lot don't miss a trick, do you?" He smiled at Lucy. "But you know what? I wouldn't have it any other way. It's good to be back."

"Of course it is. You're back with us. And wait till Gran and Pop get home, we'll all be here."

Sebastian tried not to roll his eyes, but Lucy nudged him. "I saw that. Now put me out of my misery. Who did you bring home with you? A new woman on the scene? Someone you met in Italy?"

"Well, she's Italian." He teased them by stringing the story out. "But you already know her."

"Come on, Seb. Who?" Lucy laughed.

"Isabella Romano."

"Bella from high school? Fabulous! She's back in town?"

"Just for six weeks. She's visiting her dad. And did any of you know that Con is not really Con, but Leonardo?"

The laughter around the table as Sebastian related the story of Isabella kissing him at the airport settled him even more. The half-grown wheat in the paddocks took on an orange hue as the sun slipped lower in the sky. The occasional lazy sound of a beast bellowing as dusk settled was peaceful. Even the zapping of the insects against the purple light on the edge of the verandah added to the country ambience.

Sebastian sat back and let the serenity soothe him as the happy voices washed over him. His eyelids were heavy and he almost nodded off a couple of times.

"Come on," Lucy called out. "It's time to clear up and let this poor international traveller get some sleep."

He jumped up, instantly awake. "I'll help you clean up."

"I've made up your old room for you, Seb." Jemima leaned down to give Willow a scrap of leftover meat as she scraped the plates into the bin.

"Thanks, Jemmy, you needn't have worried. I probably would have crashed on top of the bed."

"You do look tired, Seb. But happy, too."

"I am."

"Will that last out here, do you think?" Jemima had always read him well, and she cut straight to the chase as she followed him into the kitchen. "How do you think you'll cope with being home for good? You are here to stay, right?"

"Yes, I am. It's time to do my bit. I'll be fine. I'm looking forward to working with Liam."

Why did his family always think he wouldn't measure up? Sebastian covered his disappointment with a smile and picked up a tea towel. Lucy chattered away as she washed the dishes and he dried until Liam called him out to the verandah.

"I've got a favour to ask, Seb." Liam looked awkward and Sebastian frowned as he wandered out to the verandah. Ned was over in the hayshed with the children, and it was deserted out there.

What now?

"I was wondering...I was hoping," Liam cleared his throat, "that you'll agree to be my best man at the wedding."

Sebastian smiled. "I'd be honoured, mate. But what about the wedding photos? I thought you'd want me to take them?"

"Maybe you can do both? Be best man at the ceremony, and take the photos the rest of the time? For the formal group photos, I've got the photographer from the paper in town lined up."

"Sounds like it's all under control."

Angie walked out and raised her eyebrows to Liam and he nodded. "Hey, we have a best man, babe."

She hugged Sebastian. "Thank you, it means a lot to Liam."

"So tell me about the wedding? A double one, I hear?"

"Yes, last Saturday in September. It's going to be a big do here at Prickle Creek Farm We've booked a caterer from

Dubbo, one who does the event organisation and the setup and cleanup, too, so it won't be too much of a chore. When Ned and Jemmy got married in autumn, they had a civil ceremony at the registry office."

"You'll never guess who their witnesses were," Liam interjected. "Mr. and Mrs. McGillicuddy. Remember our kindergarten teacher!"

"And they want to have a proper wedding, now. So we decided on a double wedding with a celebrant, and we're going to have the reception here in the hayshed. Gran and Pop should be home a couple of weeks before the wedding because they want to go to the anniversary race meeting at Come-by-Chance." Angie smiled as she took Liam's arm. "I haven't been to a bush race meeting yet, and even though it's close to the wedding, we wouldn't miss it."

"It's going to be a busy couple of weeks. I loved those races when I was a kid."

"We all did. And this year it's the seventieth anniversary so it's a special one. I'm going to hire a small bus so we can all go out together," Liam said.

Sebastian looked out over the garden where the children were playing hide-and-seek with Ned. The family had grown since Gran had called them all home two years ago.

Certainty that he was on the right path began to move slowly through him.

All he had to do was prove himself. There was no luck involved in his international success as a photographer. He'd worked hard and he was damn good at what he did.

But now it was time to transfer that work ethic to the family farm. And prove to himself—and maybe the family—that he was capable.

It was going to be okay.

As he walked into the living room, he stopped dead and stared at the wall.

Bloody heck.

One of his photographs of a Pilliga sunset had been blown up and framed. The light played beautifully over the waving wheat as a thunderstorm built up in the west. The purple and gold contrasted with the yellow of the paddock. He remembered he'd stopped his bike and snapped off a dozen photos on his way home from town last time he'd been here. He'd texted a couple to Jemima and then forgotten about them.

Now the framed photograph, taking pride of place in the living room, brought back a memory of that awesome light. It almost filled the wall above the low cabinet that held Gran's good dinner set. He stood there for a moment before he shook his head.

"Gran got that done for Pop last Christmas. She saw the photo on my phone when you sent it to me." Jemima came through from the kitchen, carrying a couple of clean casserole dishes filled with leftovers.

"Did she know it was one of mine?" Seb reached over and took the dishes from her. "Where do these go?"

"Out to my car, please. And of course she did."

"Why would she have one of *my* photos up on the wall?"

Jemima stared at him. "Are you for real? She's really proud of you, Seb."

"I don't think so. This is Gran we're talking about."

"Listen to me. Before they went away last time, they had a few friends over, and she brought them all inside to show them the photo." Jemima folded her arms and leaned back against the doorframe as she looked at the photograph. "'My grandson, the famous photographer,' was heard quite a few times that afternoon."

Sebastian grinned and headed for the door. "Maybe the old dragon is mellowing in her old age."

Chapter Five

Steam from the ancient dishwasher filled the kitchen in the milk bar. Isabella pushed her hair back from her eyes and muttered as she pulled out the still-hot dishes. Her hair had bunched up into tight ringlets and perspiration trickled down her neck. Shirley, the woman who usually helped Dad out over the busy lunchtime rush—um, what lunchtime rush?—had rushed to the local school because her son had fallen from the playground equipment. When her father had gone to call in a casual waitress, Isabella had shaken her head.

"No, Dad. I can help you out. Goodness knows, I've done it all before."

And it would keep the mind-numbing boredom at bay. The town had changed since she and Mum had left eight years ago. Businesses had closed, and the facades of some of the shops looked neglected. Paint peeled around the once shiny display windows that were now papered over with old newspapers. Tubs with shrivelled brown plants leaned drunkenly against some of the verandah posts. It was sad to see, but it seemed self-perpetuating; as stores and businesses closed, even more shops closed when fewer people came into town to shop. She'd tried to raise the viability of the milk bar with Dad last night. Each time she'd wandered down from the apartment upstairs through the day—there were only so many hours a day you could browse restaurants and menus on the web—the milk bar had been empty. A couple of older women had bought a takeaway coffee the first time she'd come down, and when she'd ventured back down at the end of school hours, expecting to see the milk bar full of kids for an after-school drink, the shop had been completely empty.

As had the main street.

After she washed the dishes, Isabella counted the customers that came into the milk bar for the next hour as she wiped down the benches and tidied the refrigerators. She hated sitting still and not having anything to do. Dad sat at a table reading magazines. She didn't know how he put up with this, day in, day out.

"Do most people go into Narrabri to shop now?" she asked later that afternoon as Dad stood at the refrigerator in the small kitchenette in the apartment. Isabella looked around; the apartment looked smaller than when she had lived here, and the general neglect of the main street seemed to have crept in here as well.

Then again, maybe it was the lack of a feminine touch.

Dad shrugged. "I don't know. I don't ask them, Bella. I'm just happy when they come in."

"There weren't many customers today."

He waved his hand around in a very Italian gesture. "Enough to keep me busy."

She very much doubted that.

"But now that you're home, it will all be good."

And how did he come to that conclusion?

"Dad?"

"Yes, Bella?"

"What would you say if I suggested you went back to Italy for a while?"

"Now why would I want to do that? Now that you're home?"

"I'm only here six weeks."

His face fell. "I thought once you came home you might change your mind?"

Isabella shook her head emphatically. "I told you I have a new job in England."

"So you'll go and I'll be all alone again." His voice was resigned.

"Dad, I'm all grown up now. With a life of my own. Why don't you go and visit Mum?" She took a deep breath for courage. "She'd love to see you. She misses you, you know. Very much."

"If she missed me so much, she wouldn't be over there." The rigid straightness of Dad's back warned her that his volcanic temper was simmering, so she changed the subject very quickly.

"Anyway, let me tell you all about my new job."

Once his temper had subsided, Isabella knew it wasn't worth raising the subject again. It was obvious Dad was unhappy here by himself. In fact, in a few of their phone conversations over the past few months, she had even worried that he was suffering from depression.

She had six weeks to work on him, and she was determined to convince him it was time to leave Spring Downs.

I can do it. Of that she had no doubt, but it was going to take some talking.

As they were about to start preparing dinner, there was a tap on the door that led out to the alleyway next to the milk bar.

Her father frowned. "Are you expecting anyone?"

"No." Isabella shook her head. "You?"

"I never get visitors." The loneliness in Dad's voice almost brought tears to her eyes.

"Well then." She stood and headed across to the stairs. "It looks like someone's come to visit."

• • •

Late in the afternoon when they'd been working together in the shed, Liam had asked Sebastian if he'd go into town and pick up some hay.

"The produce store stays open late on Friday nights. Till six."

"Yeah, okay. I'll go now."

"Great farmer you'll make, wonder boy." Liam stood there with a grin on his face as Sebastian felt in his back pocket for his wallet and crossed the shed to pick up his helmet.

"What?" Sebastian frowned. Maybe he'd visit Isabella while he was in town, see if she wanted to go out for a spin on the bike. He knew a pretty waterhole just west of town where there was a brilliant view of the sun going down through the willows. He'd grab his camera, too.

"Hay?" Liam shook his head as Sebastian stood there with a frown on his face. "Mate, you'll need to take Pop's ute. I don't think you'll get even one hay bale on your bike." He burst out laughing. "Sorry, you should see the expression on your face."

Sebastian laughed sheepishly. "I'm going to have to get my own ute. That old rattle trap of Pop's is disgusting."

"Serves the purpose." Liam was still smiling. "Did you have other plans while you were in town?"

"Maybe. I might call into the club for a drink. See if any of my old mates are still in town." He put his helmet back on the bench at the back of the shed. "I might go and see how

Isabella's settled in while I'm there, too."

The smirk on Liam's face had reminded him of when they'd been at high school, and Sebastian had been the junior tagging along behind Liam and his friends.

He took Pop's ute into town, loaded the hay at the produce store, and when he'd finished there he drove past the RSL club, but the car park was deserted.

Not a lot happening there yet. It was probably still too early for the Friday night drinks. He parked the car in the deserted main street outside Con's Milk Bar.

Sebastian knocked on the side door and waited. Disappointment filled him when there was no answer. He tipped his head to the side. He was sure he'd heard voices upstairs. He raised his hand to knock again just as the door opened and Isabella peeked around.

"Hello." The smile that lit up her face sent warmth spiralling through him.

It was great to see her again. For the last three days since he'd been home, he kept telling himself that he had to stop thinking about her. She'd only be here a few weeks, and then she'd be heading off to England.

"Sebastian," she said. "Come on in. Dad was just saying he doesn't get many visitors."

He followed her, appreciating the cute bottom that was at eye level as she preceded him up the stairs. Or the tanned legs in the cute little pink shorts.

"Dad, do you remember Sebastian?"

"Of course I do. It's only been three days since he dropped you off. You think I'm losing the plot? Is that why you've come home?"

He held his hand out to Con as Isabella shook her head. "Good to see you again, Con." He couldn't think of him as Leonardo.

"Coffee, Sebastian? We were just about to have one.

Bella makes the best brew, don't you, *cara mia?*"

"That'd be great, thank you."

He followed Con as the older man gestured towards the sofa. "You sit there and Bella can sit beside you after she makes our coffee." Con took the single chair in front of the old television set. "Now tell me all about your plans. I hear you've come back to Prickle Creek Farm to stay."

"I have. Time to give Liam a bit of a break and help him out."

"Harry will be pleased to have his two grandsons home. And his granddaughters." Con turned and bellowed in the direction of the kitchen. "You hear that, Bella. Sebastian has come home to stay."

"I'm very pleased for him." Isabella came in juggling a tray with three cups, a coffee pot, a milk jug, and a sugar basin. Sebastian jumped up and took the tray from her.

"Thank you."

"Where would you like me to put it?"

"On the coffee table, please." As she bent and cleared away a stack of newspapers, a couple of pens, and an old TV guide, he tried to avoid looking at the neat little curves beneath her snug T-shirt. As he turned away he intercepted a look, and a satisfied smile, from Con.

A calculating, crafty look. The sort of look that Lucy got on her face when she decided to meddle in someone's life.

Con stood and waved his hand. "No coffee for me, Bella. I just remembered that I promised I'd play darts in the competition at the RSL club tonight. They were one short." He smoothed his hands over his sparse hair and winked at Sebastian. "Don't wait up for me. I'll be late."

"What about dinner?" Isabella's mouth dropped open as she stared at her father's back.

The door closed behind him, and Sebastian snuck a glance at Isabella. Her fair cheeks had twin spots of colour high on each side.

"I always seem to be putting you in embarrassing situations, don't I?" She shook her head with a smile. "The old rogue!"

"What's he up to?" Sebastian had a fair idea.

"You've come home to stay, and you came to visit, so he immediately conjures up a romance that will make me stay in town with him. I'm sorry."

He laughed. "Nothing to be sorry about."

"Oh yes." Even though she looked cross, she laughed with him. "You don't know my father. He'll have me married with six *bambinos* running around before you can take a breath. He's stubborn and determined, and when he makes up his mind about something he won't leave it alone until he gets what he wants." She flopped onto the sofa beside Sebastian. "Believe me, I understand how his mind works because I'm exactly the same." Her laugh was pretty and soft. "He taught me everything I know about no compromising. So it's game on." She looked up at him as she picked up the coffee pot. "Now back to business. Why did you call in?"

After Con's reaction and Isabella's response, he thought carefully about his reply. "I was in town and I thought I'd swing by and see how you were settling in."

She flopped back on the sofa beside him and tipped her head back. "You want the truth. I honestly don't know how I'm going to see it through. I'm going to do my best to make Dad see reason and close up shop. As soon as I can, maybe even get him to fly to Europe with me. I'll leave a bit earlier and go to Italy with him. It's so quiet here. He hardly had any customers today."

Sebastian frowned. "That's a shame. And it's Friday, too."

"What's Friday got to do with it?" As she leaned forward, her pretty lemony fragrance drifted around him, reminding him of a trip he'd taken to the Amalfi coast for a photo shoot last month.

"Everyone comes to town on Fridays. That's what the old farmers do. They come to town to pay their bills, go to the bank, the wives do the groceries, and then they go to the club for dinner."

She shook her head. "Maybe when you were a kid. But I can swear there were very few people in town today. Besides, there's no bank anymore. I noticed a sign on the door saying it had shut down a couple of weeks ago."

"Damn, that's a shame. The town really is dying. It's a fair drive to Narrabri or Dubbo to get to a bank." Sebastian wondered how long the town would survive at the rate that businesses were closing. What would be next? The school? The hospital?

"Anyway, things are okay with me. The time will fly, even if I am here for six weeks." Isabella's voice broke into his thoughts. "I've had a couple of long chats to Dad already, and it's great to see him again. It's been a couple of years since I last saw him. He met me in Bali for a holiday."

"So you haven't been back to town since you left?"

She shook her head. "You?"

"Just a handful of visits." He finished his coffee and looked at her. "How about we go out for a drink? See some of the sights of town."

She chuckled. "That'd be quick. Where to?"

"Is there a choice?" he said with a smile.

"Okay, I guess the RSL club it is. Maybe we can cheer Dad on at darts." She stood and looked down at him. "Have another coffee while I get changed."

Sebastian looked around the small apartment as he poured another coffee. It was a bland room with only basic furniture, and he imagined how boring it would be to be stuck in here all day. At least at Gran's house, he had plenty of room and a large-screen television. He grinned to himself. Even if he did have to put up with all of her ornaments and crocheted doilies and the overpowering smell of moth balls each time he opened the cupboard for a fresh towel.

His phone buzzed in his pocket and he pulled it out, glancing curiously at the screen. It was Liam.

"What's up, mate. I've got the hay, and the produce store is shut now so it's too late to get anything else you've thought of."

"No. Something else has come up. I came home to an upset Angie, and then Jemima."

Sebastian sat up straight and frowned. "Everyone okay? Are the kids all right?"

"Yeah, yeah. Everyone's fine. I was hoping you had caught up with Isabella."

"I have. We're about to go to the club for a drink. Maybe dinner."

He didn't know if Isabella would fancy a bistro meal.

"Would you mind if we came in and joined you?" Liam asked.

"You and Angie?"

"And Ned and Jemmy and the kids."

Sebastian nodded. "That's fine. The more the merrier. What about Lucy and Garth?"

"This is a wedding problem. But I'll give them a call. I'm sure Lucy would love to catch up with Isabella."

"Okay. We'll grab a big table."

"See you in an hour or so. Thanks, Seb. And I hope we're not cramping your style too much, lover boy."

Sebastian shook his head as he put the phone back into his pocket. *Lover boy!* He should be so lucky.

He stood as Isabella came back into the small living room. He was pleased she hadn't overdressed because he'd only changed into a clean pair of black jeans and a clean

T-shirt before he'd driven into town. Her jeans were dark like his, and she had a short-sleeved T-shirt with *I Love Roma* on the front, inside a big pink heart.

"Me, too," he said with a grin.

She glanced down at the heart and his eyes followed hers.

"The food is to die for there. Lots of quirky little restaurants in alleyways, and you never know what celebrity you're going to run into."

"*Hmm.* I hope the local bistro measures up food-wise, but I can't promise you a celebrity."

Her laugh tinkled around him, but he stood still as she walked closer and put her hand on the front of his shirt. "You know what, Sebastian?"

He loved the way her accent lilted on his name. "What should I know?"

She lifted her other hand and cupped his cheek. "You worry too much. It will be fine."

He ignored the zing that rushed through him as her hand touched his face. "I hope so." He smiled as he held her gaze, and the look they shared sent another zing through him.

Slow down, boy.

"Liam rang when you were getting changed. It's turned into a party. The whole family's coming into town for dinner."

"Lucy, too?"

He nodded.

"Oh, that's great." Her smile was wide, and he held out his hand.

"Come on, we'll go and fight with the crowds at the local rissole."

Chapter Six

Sebastian kept hold of Isabella's hand as they strolled down to the local RSL club at the end of the main street. It was just like being back at school and hanging out in town. Of course, in those days, it had been her father's milk bar that had been the hangout place, and no one had been game to hold her hand in those days, in case her dad had seen them.

Isabella groaned and rolled her eyes as she spotted her father having a cigarette out on the front lawn with a couple of his friends. Of course, he spotted straight away that Sebastian was holding her hand.

Round one to Dad. There'd be no stopping him now.

The club was surprisingly busy, and she stood next to Sebastian as he signed in as a visitor.

"I guess now that I'm a local again, I'll have to join the club and pay my fees."

"You really are serious about staying here now, aren't you?" She looked at him quizzically. "What about your photographic career?"

"On hold for the time being. And yes, I have to stay here."

"Why *have* to?"

Before he answered, her father walked in behind them. His smile was wide, and he winked as he walked past her into the games room.

She followed Sebastian across to the bar area, and they perched on two high stools where they could see the game of darts underway.

"Might as well give him something to look back at," she said with a resigned sigh, after Sebastian had ordered their drinks.

"You should be happy your father wasn't at the airport when you jumped on me."

"Oh *Dio,* yes. That would have made his day. He'd have you shopping for engagement rings by now!"

"Poor man. All he wants is to have his lovely daughter home with him."

"I know." Isabella reached for her drink. "I do feel a bit guilty. I'm sad for him, but if he's not happy here, or if he's lonely here—and I know he is—it's up to him to do something about it. The guilt trip won't work on me. He got me home for a visit and that's all he's going to get."

Sebastian looked around the club. Most of the tables were full, but he'd reserved a table in the dining room for seven o'clock for dinner for when the mob arrived. "It's not that bad," he said slowly. "I think the comparison you—and me, too—are making at the moment is because we've been living somewhere perceived as exotic by most of the population. But look,"—Isabella looked down as he reached along the bar and took her head and squeezed it—"is it really so different?"

She followed his gaze and looked around the club, conscious of the warmth of his fingers as they held hers. Young couples with small children sat in groups, chatting and laughing, just like you'd see in any Italian square. The games room was full of older men, arguing and joking over the darts game. A game of carpet bowls was under way in the far corner, and it reminded her of the old men playing *bocce* on the grass outside her tiny apartment in Santo Spirito. An apartment, if she was honest, that was much smaller than her father's in Spring Downs.

She nodded slowly and looked down at their hands joined on the bar. "I get what you're saying. I guess people are the same the world over. It doesn't matter where you live." She lifted her eyes to his and was struck by the intensity of his gaze. This was getting way too serious all of a sudden. She pulled her hand away and picked up her drink again. "But the bottom line is I don't want to live here. Can you understand that?"

"Of course I can. It's different for me, because I own a quarter share in a ten-thousand-acre property. I guess I own the cattle and the wheat, too." She smiled as he shook his head. "I haven't got my head around that yet. I'm still getting used to being back here."

He lifted his beer, and she watched the muscles in his strong throat work as he swallowed. Maybe it was just as well they hadn't met in Florence. Isabella had a feeling that she could really like Sebastian.

"So any local celebrities in here tonight?" she asked playfully.

He looked around and then leaned over, and his warm breath brushed her ear.

Not what I'm trying to do. She was altogether too aware of him already. His leg was hard up against hers as he leaned in to answer. "Promise you won't go all fangirl on me?"

"I promise," she said with a giggle. "Who's here? Did you bring your camera?"

"I did." He lowered his voice. "It's Wally Sykes. The shire president."

She pretended to fan herself. "Oh, be still my beating

heart."

"And to answer your question, my camera is always with me; however, I left it in the car."

"Is it safe to do that here?"

Sebastian nodded. "Spring Downs Shire might be boring, but one of the advantages of it not being a hive of happening, means it has the lowest crime rate in New South Wales."

Isabella couldn't help herself and burst out laughing. "A hive of happening? What is that?"

He looked a bit sheepish. "You know. Hip, trendy, and all those things, but I think the era surrounding us might understand the term 'groovy' a bit more."

"The decor of the club is certainly groovy." She gestured to the royal blue curtains that hung either side of the raised stage and then jumped to her feet as the main door of the club opened.

"Lucy. Over here," Isabella called as she hurried over to the door. When she reached Lucy, they embraced for a moment. Isabella looked at the tall man standing behind Lucy holding a toddler. "Oh my God, Luce! I didn't know you married Garth. You're Lucy Mackenzie now?"

"I did and I am. It's so good to see you, Bella." Lucy nodded as Isabella reached up and kissed Garth's cheek. "I remember when she used to pretend you were married and scrawled Lucy Mackenzie in hearts in all her school books."

"Don't give away all my secrets." Lucy took her arm as Sebastian gestured to the dining room. "Come on. We've got a table booked in there. Where are the others?"

"Ned is just parking the car. They won't be long."

They chatted nonstop as they made their way to the dining room. Sebastian came over and waited till there was break in the conversation.

"Drinks? Lucy, wine?"

"No thanks, I'm the designated driver tonight. I'll have

a squash, please." Lucy turned to Garth. "Here, honey, pass James to me and go and help Seb. You might as well get a couple of jugs of soft drink because the McCormack kids are on the way in."

Isabella watched as the two men headed back to the bar and then turned back to Lucy who was looking at her curiously. Her cheeks heated as she picked up the meaning in Lucy's expression, and she shook her head.

"We're just friends, so don't go getting any of your ideas. I remember what you were like, setting people up in high school. It's bad enough that I've got Dad on my case."

"I didn't say a word," Lucy objected. "Anyway, this is James. Say hello to Aunty Bella, James."

The little boy was more interested in the car he held in his pudgy hand than any new adult, and Isabella leaned back in her chair with a smile. "I'm so pleased you came into town tonight. I was going to ring you tomorrow," she said.

"We had to. There's been a drama, but I'll let the other girls tell you about it."

By the time Sebastian and Garth had come back with two trays of drinks, glasses, and jugs, the others had arrived and Isabella was introduced to Angie and Ned. She didn't remember Ned from school, and Liam had changed so much she wouldn't have recognised him.

Angie and Jemima sat on either side of Isabella after asking Lucy to move up one place.

Once the children were settled and the noise level had decreased a few decibels, Jemima leaned in closer.

"Isabella, we have a huge, huge favour to ask you. If you don't feel comfortable or you can't do it, we'll totally understand, but we're well and truly stuck."

"Actually desperate," Angie said. "We're so disappointed, but at least we haven't lost any money."

Isabella shook her head, bemused. "You'd better explain,

because I have no idea what you mean."

"Didn't Seb tell you?"

She shook her head again.

Jemima rolled her eyes. "That man hasn't changed a bit since he was a little boy. He always sits back and lets things happen."

Isabella straightened in her chair. That was a bit unfair to Seb. The poor guy had only just arrived back in town. And besides he'd been very kind to her, and she didn't like to hear him criticised.

Angie leaned in closer as the band on the stage began to play a jazz piece. "Do you want to go and sit at the tables outside? It's cooled down a bit."

"Sure. I'll just tell Sebastian where I'm going."

She ignored the glance that passed between them. It was only the polite thing to do. Sebastian had brought her here, and she didn't want him to think she was leaving without him.

Five minutes later a light breeze was cooling them in the barbeque area at the back of the club, although the west-facing brick wall still held the heat from the sun. It had been a brilliantly clear day, although apart from a short stroll along the main street, Isabella had stayed out of the hot sun. She'd forgotten how dry the heat was out here in the Pilliga, and it would only get hotter before she left at the end of October. Turning up in England in the middle of autumn would be a shock after summer in Florence, and then half the down under spring in Australia. She turned to the two women opposite her.

"Okay, gals. Now tell me what this drama is and how you think I can help."

Jemima was the first to talk. "We were all organised for the wedding." Then she looked at Isabella. "Did Seb tell you we're having a double wedding at Prickle Creek Farm on the last Saturday in September?"

"He mentioned it at the airport. Yes."

"We were all organised. Celebrant, dresses, suits, kids' outfits, and caterer." Jemima rolled her eyes. "And then this afternoon, we got a call from the catering company. They've gone bust, and luckily they hadn't cashed our deposit cheque so we were able to put a stop on it."

"We've spent the whole afternoon ringing caterers, and even mobile roast vans, but everyone is booked with summer coming up," Angie said.

Jemima reached up and pushed her hair back from her eyes as a gust of hot wind blew in from the west. "We even considered having it here at the club, but neither of us wants a reception in town."

"We thought about changing the weekend, but then we're getting too close to Jemmy's due date." Angie glanced over at Jemima's tummy.

"So," Isabella said with a smile. "You're going to ask me if—"

"If you'll cater for a wedding in Gran's hayshed for more than a hundred guests," Angie rushed the words out.

"I'd love to," she said simply.

"Really?" Angie squealed and Jemima smiled.

"You've got yourselves a deal, and you've saved me from wondering what the hell I was going to do for the next few weeks."

"Oh, Isabella that is awesome." As the girls rushed back inside to share the news, Isabella followed slowly. Sebastian was looking at her, and she smiled as she caught his eye.

The meal was a happy occasion, and she was aware of him sitting beside her. It was the only time in the whole night that there was relative quiet. The conversations quieted and the band took a break just before the meals were served.

"When are you going to come out to the farm and check out the venue?" Sebastian pushed away his plate and leaned close to her. "You've really stepped in and saved the day. The girls are really happy."

"I just hope I don't disappoint," she said. "I've always had help when I've done big functions in the restaurant."

"Oh, don't worry about that. When Gran gets home, she'll mobilise the CWA ladies. You'll have an army of helpers. Your job is the food." He held her eyes with his deep brown ones and a delicious little shiver ran down her back. "And I'll have company when you're out there getting everything ready."

"Aren't your grandparents coming home soon?" she asked. "I thought I heard Jemima say they would be home in the next week or so."

The frown on his face surprised her.

"That soon?" he said and then must have thought better of it. "That'll be nice."

Isabella wondered why he sounded unimpressed.

Chapter Seven

Sebastian had been disappointed the night before when Isabella's father had walked back to the milk bar with them. His disappointment had been tempered by her promise to borrow her father's car and come out to see the hayshed and check out Gran's kitchen.

Jemima and Angie were coming over to discuss the menu and what they wanted to happen on the afternoon of the wedding. Sebastian smiled as he unloaded the hay from the ute and put it just inside the door of the shed. No point taking it over near the tractor where it usually went, if this shed was going to be turned into a reception centre.

Isabella had offered to step in as event coordinator, too.

With her helping out at the wedding, he'd get to see a lot more of her. As he carried the last bale into the shed, his phone buzzed in his pocket. He threw the hay on top of the pile and pulled his phone out.

"Sebastian Richards."

"Seb, it's Chris."

"Hey mate, how's it going?"

Chris was his agent, and he'd been trying to talk Sebastian out of coming back to the farm for the past three months. Sebastian knew he was worried about losing his big fat commission if Sebastian stopped selling photos.

"Where are you?" Chris asked. "Out in the boondocks yet?"

"Yes, I'm at the *farm*. Been here since Tuesday. Where are you?"

"That's good. I'm in Sydney and I've got a job for you."

Sebastian ran his hand through his hair impatiently. "Chris, I already told you. I'm not available to take off around the world at the drop of a hat."

"You don't have to go anywhere with this job. Well, not far, anyway."

"What are you talking about?"

"Grimes and Haines called me when they heard you were back in the country, and mate, this job has fallen in your lap. It's perfect for you!"

The excitement in Chris's voice spread to Sebastian. He loved that little flare of anticipation that fired when a new shoot was first discussed, but he pushed it away. He was on the farm now; his days of being a photographer were over.

But it wouldn't hurt to ask what he was going to miss out on. "Tell me about it."

"It's a calendar series. They want day and night shots of the sky and the landscape."

"What landscape?" He could hear the anticipation in Chris's voice as he reeled him in. His agent was a crafty bugger; he knew exactly how to get Sebastian interested.

"The bloody Outback, mate. Right on your doorstep."

"What's the time frame?" Okay, so he was taking the bait a bit too quickly.

"Two months to do it, only twelve shots, a spring and summer shoot, ready for international distribution mid-next year." Chris's words kept bubbling over. "And mate, the calendar company wants you so badly, the fee I quoted was mega and guess what?"

"What?"

"You've hit the big time. They didn't even want to negotiate. Said yes on the first call and said to get you signed up. So what do you reckon?"

"Yes."

Chris's laughter came down the phone. "You're sure you don't want to think about that some more?"

"No. I'll fit it in on weekends." The excitement had grown from a little spark to a blazing fire. He was back in the business and could do it from here.

And he had a great candidate in mind for a location assistant.

He slid the phone in his pocket and walked towards the house, his mood improving even more as the dust kicked up by the mailbox. An unfamiliar yellow sedan drove slowly along the road from the cattle grid, and he stood by the gate to the house yard, waiting for it to appear around the last turn.

He smiled when he saw Isabella hunched low over the steering wheel of an old Citroën. It had to be a 1960s model, but it was in perfect condition. He walked over and opened the door for her, and she climbed out gracefully.

"Thank you." With a laugh she ran her fingers through her curls that seemed to be springier than usual. "When Dad told me there was no air con in the car, I almost rang you to come and collect me on the bike."

"Any time. Love the car, by the way," he said. "What model is it?"

She shrugged. "I don't know. All I know is I hate driving it!"

"It's a classic." Sebastian smoothed his hand over the

shiny, canary-yellow paintwork. "Did you having any trouble finding the place?"

"No, your directions were spot on, but you *are* a long way out of town." She leaned against the car and looked around. "Your farm is beautiful. I didn't imagine there'd be a green lawn and such a pretty garden way out here in the red dirt. Even roses!"

"Gran's always been proud of her garden. Woe betide any dog or child who interferes with her plants." He followed her gaze across the colorful early spring flowers. "I don't know who's been taking care of it while they've been away but someone obviously has."

"The flowers will be great to decorate the hayshed for the wedding."

"If you need a hand with anything, make sure you ask me. I'd love to help."

"Don't worry, I will. You have a great family." Isabella's voice held a wistful note. "I really enjoyed meeting everyone again last night. I feel so old, seeing Lucy with a baby and Jemima pregnant with an instant family. Only problem was, when we got home Dad started on the 'how long till I'm a *nonno*' questions!"

"Do you want kids one day?" Sebastian asked curiously.

She shrugged. "I've been too busy building my career to think about it. Plenty of time for that in the future."

"Me, too. But I don't know that I could ever settle in one place long enough to raise a family."

She looked at him strangely and he realised what he'd just said.

"So you're not here to stay, after all?" she asked.

His laugh was forced. "I forgot for a moment that I'd come home to stay. I think I'm still jetlagged. Anyway, come on over and I'll show you the shed while we're waiting for the others to get here."

"Angie called as I turned off the road. She's on her way."

• • •

While Sebastian put the working dogs into their pens, Isabella waited at the front of the hayshed across from the pretty garden. She pulled out her phone and took some photos. She could already visualise how the big shed could be set up. Angie and Jemima had run some ideas past her, and she was looking forward to talking more about it, now that she'd seen the space where they would set up a semi-outdoor reception. As well as looking after the catering, they'd been happy to accept her offer to organise the "event" in terms of layout and decorations.

"You are a lifesaver," Jemima had said. "This pregnancy has slowed me down so much, I can barely cope looking after the house and kids, let alone plan a wedding."

Angie had nodded. "It's awesome that you are willing to do it for us. I've been busy at the vet surgery and trying to get our new house organised. You'll have to come and see it." Then she shook her head and smiled. "It's probably the last thing you want to do while you're visiting your dad. Look at paint schemes and new furniture! We'll be taking up enough of your time with the wedding organisation."

Isabella had shaken her head. "I'd love to come and visit."

"I won't be long." Sebastian locked the gate of the dog pen. "I'm just going to look for Daisy. She's disappeared. Make yourself at home."

Isabella wandered around the shed and checked out where the power points were. It would be easy to set up some food warmers and serve some of the meal from inside. Planning the menu and the table decoration would keep her busy, and she closed her eyes as she whispered a thank you to the company that had pulled out and given her this opportunity.

Her time in Spring Downs would be bearable now. She'd had to bite her tongue already, because now that Dad had got over his initial happiness at seeing her, he'd started in on her. Last night—on what was it, only her fourth night in town— she'd actually been tempted to look up an earlier flight out.

The conversation had started out pleasantly enough.

"What have you been doing in Florence?"

"Working," she'd answered patiently.

"Where have you been working?"

"In the middle of the city."

"Do you have many friends?" Of course, no mention of Mum.

"What is this job you are so excited about? Why do you have to go to England?"

And then all the negatives had followed.

"You work too hard, Bella. It's not right for a woman to work so hard. You need a man to look after you and give you babies."

That had been the comment that had almost pushed her over the edge, but she'd gritted her teeth and waved an airy hand. "Oh, there's plenty of time for that, Dad. No rush at all. There's a whole world out there, and success beckons."

"No, you're in your mid-twenties. Most women have a home and family by then."

"Not most women in my world, Dad." She'd tempered her words with a smile and changed the subject. Five more weeks of nagging from her father, in a town where there was nothing to do, had loomed.

A faint yapping at the back of the hayshed caught her attention, and she wandered across to the dark corner behind the tractor.

She drew a quick breath. A sleek red kelpie was lying in the hay with what seemed like dozens of little puppies fighting to latch on to her for a feed. She kneeled down and counted the pups.

"You must be Daisy." The mother lifted her head and tired eyes almost smiled in contentment. "What a clever girl. Nine beautiful puppies."

Isabella pushed herself to her feet and walked back outside. "Sebastian, is Daisy a kelpie?"

He came around from the back of the shed. "She is, and she's due to whelp any day."

"She's in the shed behind the tractor with her new family."

A beautiful smile crossed Sebastian's face. His full, firm lips tilted, and she remembered how they'd felt against hers. "Over there?"

"Yes, tucked in behind the back wheel."

His voice was low and soothing as he crouched down beside the bitch and her pups. "Who's a clever girl then, Miss Daisy? All by yourself without a peep."

Isabella stood beside him and watched as Sebastian patted Daisy's head. He'd thrown his hat to the straw on the ground before he'd squatted down. His hair was pulled back neatly into a tight man bun, and the leather tie holding it back today was black, the same colour as his T-shirt and jeans. He looked as far removed from a cattle farmer as he could possibly be. Without the hat, he could have walked into any coffee shop in Florence and blended into the trendy crowd. She wondered if he was really serious about making a life on the farm. It was as though Sebastian was out of the environment that suited him.

With a shrug, she turned away. It wasn't any of her business, but she certainly knew she couldn't make a life here, and she imagined it would be hard for Sebastian, after living in Italy. She turned and looked at the scenery through the wide door.

It was beautiful—in its own way. A huge expanse of

blue sky, so bright that it made her squint, stretched into the distance. The land was flat, and behind the house, golden fields of wheat stretched as far as she could see. It was a harsh and bright landscape, very different to the soft muted landscapes of the northern hemisphere.

She jumped when a warm hand touched her shoulder.

"Penny for your thoughts?" he asked. "You were miles away."

"I was just thinking how beautiful this is." She spread her hand in a wide gesture. "And quiet. Not a sound to be heard."

"A bit quieter and more peaceful than the sound of the Ferraris roaring across the bridges over the river Arno on a sleepy Sunday morning in Florence, isn't it?" He stared at the landscape, and she would have sworn his expression was wistful.

"Not to mention the noise of the market setting up outside my window before dawn every Sunday. Now that is one thing I won't miss!"

The cattle grate rattled again, and she pointed towards the gate. "Here comes a sports car, so not too different."

"It's Jemima's." Isabella had been fascinated when Lucy had told her of Jemima's international career as a fashion model before she'd come back home to take her turn helping out on the farm, and how she'd married Ned across the road to help him get a bank loan. The story of how they'd fallen in love was a beauty. As the silver Audi rattled across the cattle grid, two farm utes came in from the other side of the property.

"There's a back gate that leads to Garth and Lucy's place. It saves a long drive around the road." Sebastian leaned down, his cheek close to hers and one arm draped casually across her shoulders. "If you look directly over that wheat, the paddock where the big gum tree is, can you see a flash of silver in the distance?" He pointed to the north.

Isabella nodded, conscious of the warmth radiating from his arm to her bare skin. She'd put on a skirt and a camisole top with thin straps today, leaving her shoulders bare. Even though it was only early spring, it was still warm in the middle of the day, and she'd thought this morning it would be nice to get some colour before she headed into the cold of an English winter. A strange shiver ran down her back. She'd only have to turn her head to put her lips against his neck. He hadn't shaved this morning, and an enticing darkness tinged his strong jaw line. The kiss they'd shared—or rather the kiss she'd demanded at the airport—had been in her dreams every night since she'd arrived.

In fact, Sebastian had been in her thoughts pretty constantly over the past few days. She stepped away, cross at the direction her thoughts were taking her. It was only because they were both newly arrived in town, and they'd shared common experiences.

She frowned. He was one very attractive guy, and she'd caught his eyes thoughtfully on her a few times at the club last night. Isabella stepped forward with determination in her step. There was no point getting involved with him, no matter how tempting it was. She was here for another five weeks and three days.

"Lucy came, too," Sebastian said as he walked over to the first ute. "Now you'll get organised."

Jemima had brought Ryan, and Lucy had James on one hip. Sebastian kissed each of the women, and then put on his hat.

"I'll leave you ladies to it." He grinned and a flutter of butterflies took up residence in Isabella's tummy.

Stop it, you're not in high school now, she admonished herself.

"Give me a yell when it's cuppa time." Sebastian tipped his hat back and strode off towards the paddocks. His jeans were snug around his thighs, and she watched until he was out of sight.

Isabella turned around to see a satisfied smile on Lucy's face. The same look that her father had given her last night.

"Seb got the gene for the good looks in the family, that's for sure." Lucy winked at her.

"Don't even think about it, Lucy." She looped her arm through Lucy's spare one as Angie and Jemima headed towards the house. "You haven't changed a bit since we were at high school. I'm here for six weeks and then I'm off."

A happy sigh left Isabella's lips as the smell of spring flowers drifted around them. The next three weeks planning this wedding would be fun.

Chapter Eight

Her happy mood lasted until after dinner. Dad had been quiet and hadn't spoken much as they'd eaten the lasagne that she'd cooked when she'd come home from Prickle Creek Farm. Isabella hadn't laughed as much as she had in the kitchen at the farm this afternoon. Chatting with Lucy, Jemima, and Angie had made her realise that she had let her friendships go. Working hard in Florence had taken up most of her days, Sunday had been her only day off from the restaurant, and they were spent doing her laundry, cleaning the small apartment, and catching up with her mother. There had been little time for socialising, and most of her friends had been work colleagues, anyway. It had been a while since she'd had a good female chin wag.

Finally, Dad sat back, picked up his napkin, and wiped his mouth. "That was very good, thank you, Bella."

"I love to cook. Even when I'm not working." She reached over and touched his hand when he put the napkin down. "Are you okay, Dad? You're very quiet tonight."

He nodded sadly. "I'm okay. I'm just thinking about

when you leave, how lonely it will be again."

Luckily, she was looking at him to see the crafty look he shot her before he looked down at the table.

Two can play at this game.

"Yes, it must be very lonely for you. I think it's time you made a change." Isabella could be crafty, too. After all, she took after him. Stubborn and determined to get her own way. They'd had some doozies of arguments when she was in high school.

"Mum has been so sad lately, too," she said.

"*Hmph*," he said. "Why should she be sad and lonely? She's had you over there with her since she left. Although she tells me that you neglected her."

Neglected her? Isabella pushed away the anger that niggled and seized on the one piece of information that Dad had let drop.

"And since when have you been having conversations with Mum?"

"We talk." He sat back and folded his arms across his portly stomach.

"I didn't know that, but I'm pleased. And as you well know, I've been living in my own place for ages."

He dismissed her protest with a wave of his hand. "We talk because we worry about you. You know if you stayed here, I think your mother would come home."

This time her temper bubbled over. "Don't even think about it!"

"Think about her coming home? I thought that's what you wanted?" His tone was hurt.

"No, you know very well what I mean. Don't even think about trying to blackmail me. I'm not going to stay here on the off-chance that Mum might come back. That's between the two of you. I'm a big girl now, and I have my own life and career."

"Not much of a life, cooking for other people all day."

"Oh," she said sweetly, "and tell me what it is you do all day, Dad?"

"I'm a man. That's different."

Isabella stood and threw her napkin to the table. Two volatile Italian tempers threatened to erupt. It wouldn't be pretty if she hung around.

"I'm going for a walk. You can do the dishes. Unless that's not a man's job?" She managed not to slam the door behind her and ran down the steps. Five minutes later, she'd walked the length of the main street as she worked off her temper. Past the library and the produce store, and three empty stores on one side, across the road, and up the other side. The bakery, the butcher shop, and the local grocery store were closed and the lights were off. Two cars drove past while she was walking, and a red kelpie barked at her from the back of a ute parked outside the vet surgery. The light was on in the surgery, and for a moment, Isabella was tempted to go in and see Angie for a vent. She'd said she had a couple of late consultations. Before she pushed open the gate she changed her mind. She barely knew Angie, and it wasn't her problem.

Isabella turned and walked more slowly back the way she'd come, along past the milk bar and towards the bridge. Seeing the town so quiet and deserted made her homesick for Italy. Spring Downs wasn't home. She had only lived here for three years before Mum had headed back to Italy.

Dad should have come with them. It had hurt so much when Mum had made the decision to go, and Dad had stubbornly folded his arms and refused to budge. She passed the museum and opened the gate that led to the path that ran along the river and back to the shop.

She had thought that her dad hadn't loved her enough to come with them.

That had stayed with her for a long time until she just

forgot about it by immersing herself in work.

Her logical mind told her it wasn't her fault. The problem was between Mum and Dad, but the risk of failing them as a daughter, and thinking that she was somehow to blame for their separation, had been exacerbated by adolescent emotion and imagination.

So am I a failure as a daughter? Staying here with Dad wouldn't fix anything. Isabella had vowed to work even harder to make up for it and make a success of her career. She'd set the goal as soon as she'd qualified, and she'd worked her butt off to get there for the past eight years.

Failure was a word that could be banished by hard work.

And she'd been successful. And she would be even more successful in the new restaurant. Another promotion, another step up the ladder. One day, she would have her own place.

Only thing was she didn't know where it would be. She smiled to herself. One thing was certain; it wouldn't be in the Outback of Australia. As she turned away from the river and headed back to the alleyway at the side of the milk bar, she brushed away the single tear that escaped before she banished the hurt back down where it belonged.

Coming home to see Dad had not been a smart move.

• • •

As Sebastian parked the motorbike outside the milk bar, the security light came on in the narrow alley outside the door of the apartment. Isabella was walking in from the river side of the alley. Her mobile must be switched off, so he'd decided to come into town and see her. He jumped off, unclipping his helmet, and hurried across the footpath, calling her before she disappeared through the door.

"Isabella,'" he called again as he got closer to the door. She looked up and even in the dim light, he could see the smile on her face was wide.

Phew. He'd been worried that she might think he was being a nuisance. He'd thought long and hard about coming into town. He had no reason to, apart from seeing Isabella. It was only because it was so quiet and lonely at the farm. Liam had gone back to his own house not long after the three girls had left. Sebastian had decided not to go in for afternoon tea. It had been wedding planning time, and he would've just been in the way. Besides, Liam had left a list of jobs and he'd not got through them all. By the time he'd fixed the gate in the side fence over near the calf paddock, red dust had hung in the air over the driveway and he'd cursed himself. Isabella had left and he hadn't had a chance to say goodbye.

He'd stood at the chest freezer in Gran's laundry for a couple of minutes, pulled out a plastic container labeled CURRIED CHICKEN, and thawed it in the microwave. He'd flicked the news on while he ate, but it hadn't held his interest. Then he'd even stood at the fridge and thought about a beer, but he hadn't really felt like one, after all.

Somehow, Sebastian found himself on his bike and halfway to town, his camera safely in the pannier before he'd thought it through.

"Sebastian?" Isabella walked toward him, pulling a light cardigan around her shoulders. The chill air had descended as soon as the sun had gone down. "What are you doing in town?"

"I've got some news," he said. "And maybe another job for you if you're interested. I tried to call but your phone went straight to voicemail."

"The battery's flat. I put it onto charge when I came home from the farm, and I forgot about it."

"Had dinner?"

"Yep. I've been out for a walk," she replied.

"Want to come for a ride? I've got some places I need to

see."

"Really? At night?" Isabella did up a couple of buttons of her cardigan.

He laughed. "Did that sound like a pickup line?"

He was relieved when she laughed back with him. He really didn't know her well enough yet to read her body language, but she'd seemed a little bit preoccupied as she'd walked towards him.

"I guess it's more original than come up and see my etchings, but yes, I'd love to come for a ride."

He grinned as relief filled him. "Hey, I usually say 'come up and see my photographs.' Works like a treat every time."

"Original. Wait here. I'll just run up and put some jeans on and tell Dad I'm going out." Her laugh was soft. "If you come up, we'll never get away."

As Sebastian waited, he pulled his camera out of the pannier. The moon was low in the sky, and the soft light illuminating the tired facades of the stores was perfect.

Click, click. He'd adjust the raw images to sepia; that would capture the forlorn deserted atmosphere perfectly. It was great to have his camera in hand again. By the time he'd taken a couple of dozen more shots and put the camera away, Isabella was standing on the footpath beside him, pulling on a leather jacket. Putting the camera down, Sebastian lifted the spare helmet and passed it to her.

"Can you take photos when it's this dark? Without a flash?"

He nodded. "Sure can. Special night lens."

"I don't know anything about cameras. My limit is the camera on my phone." She climbed on the bike behind him, and he smiled as her hands grasped his waist. A ripple of pleasure ran down his back and settled warmly in his gut as he started the bike and it let out a muted roar.

"We're even then. I don't know anything about cooking."

"Where are we off to?"

"A surprise."

Half an hour west of town was an old cattle property that Liam had said was abandoned. A long railway bridge crossed the river about a kilometre past the derelict house, and Sebastian had it in mind for one of the calendar shots. As he'd worked today, he'd thought of the places locally where he didn't have to travel far to get good night shots, but he knew he'd have to go farther afield to get a suitable portfolio of day photographs together. It was going to have to be on the weekends since there was a lot of work to do on the property. A lot more than he'd ever imagined. He couldn't leave Liam to it through the week. It wouldn't be the right thing to do, and he could just imagine the look—and the comment—he'd get if he said he was taking the day off to take some photos.

Talking to Liam this morning had been an eye-opener. The wheat harvest was coming up, Liam had increased the herd size, and there was a lot of cattle work ahead before summer came.

"I'm pleased you came home when you did. I would have had to hire another couple of blokes," he'd said as they stopped for smoko this morning. "Now that the place is ours, I think with you being here, and having a couple of extra hands when it gets busy, we can make Prickle Creek one of the showcase farms in the district."

Sebastian had been surprised, but he'd not commented. The time would come when he and Liam had to align their visions of what the farm meant to each of them. Sebastian was happy to go along as Pop always had, running the place as a going concern, but not as a showcase farm.

But that's Liam for you. He'd always been a high achiever and wanted to be the best of everything he took on. And that was where a lot of the comments about Sebastian being the "lucky one" had been rooted. To give him credit, Liam had worked hard for his success in the newspaper world, and it looked like he was about to apply the same work philosophy to the farm. Although Liam had to remember it was a jointly owned family business now.

He'd give it a few weeks, get the wedding out of the way, and then before Gran and Pop headed off again, they'd have a meeting.

A shareholders' meeting. If Liam wanted the farm to be a showcase business, they'd have to put the family ties aside and treat it as a company. Sebastian had a feeling that there was going to be some conflict ahead. He wanted the farm to be a success as much as Liam did, but not at the cost of his time to pursue his photography on weekends. No matter what Liam declared, Sebastian had no intention of working seven days a week.

He indicated to turn right just before the Come-by-Chance turnoff, headed down the bumpy dirt road, past the deserted Paterson farm and along to the clearing by the river. Isabella put her head closer to his as they passed a couple of signs, but they'd flashed past before he'd been able to read them. The farmhouse was in darkness and it looked abandoned. Rusted machinery littered the paddock by the house, and the grass was long and unkempt. The front gate hung crookedly from a dilapidated fence.

Absolutely perfect!

Everywhere he looked, there was a photographic subject, and his certainty that this Outback series was going to be spectacular increased every time he looked around.

A kilometre down the road he pulled the bike up and lifted his visor with a satisfied grunt. The light was bloody perfect. He climbed off, helped Isabella off, and opened the pannier.

"Bear with me for a second." Pulling the lens cap off, he shoved it in his pocket and switched the camera on before he ran through the long grass to the edge of the river. Giving a fleeting thought to snakes—no, it was too early in the season—he lay on his stomach in the grass. The moon was positioned perfectly behind the branches of an old white ghost gum and in the foreground were the ruins of an old shed. The shutter clicked as he turned the camera from side to side, and it was only a minute or so later that a drift of cloud obscured the moon.

Just got it in time.

He pushed himself to his feet, and the dry leaves rustled as he walked back to the bike. Isabella had wandered to a stand of weeping willows, and she was staring out across the narrow channel of water. He couldn't help himself; he lifted the camera and clicked. It would be a nice shot to have as a memory when she left.

Sebastian frowned. The thought of her leaving didn't sit well with him. In less than a week, he'd really gotten used to Isabella being here and being such a part of the place. It wasn't as though they'd been friends at school, but he liked being around her.

"Sorry about that. I knew the light wouldn't last." He walked over to stand beside her.

With a smile, she turned to face him. "No problem. I simply appreciate being out here. It's a beautiful night."

"Is everything okay?" He hesitated before he continued. "You seem a bit preoccupied. You're not having second thoughts about the wedding after talking to the girls, are you?"

"Oh no. I'm really excited about that." She reached up and pushed her curls away from her face. "Just family stuff. Dad's being painful. Carrying on about me staying here. I should have been prepared for it. I'd forgotten what he's like."

"What would you do here? I mean what does *he* think you'd do here?"

She looked at him for a moment before she answered, and it was hard to read her expression. "Get married and have babies, probably."

"He's a bit old school?"

"Yep, that and lonely. He should go home."

"Home?"

"To Italy, but he's so damn stubborn, he won't give in to common sense. Unless Dad thinks it's his idea, accepting anyone else's idea is a weakness to him, and he won't even discuss it."

"It's a generational trait, I think." Sebastian held out his hand. "Come on, we'll walk along the river for a while, and I'll let you in on one of my deep, dark secrets."

"Ooh, sounds intriguing." Isabella curled her fingers around his.

"I've got a couple of things to tell you, actually." Sebastian adjusted the camera strap around his neck so he could walk closer to her.

"Good or bad?"

"I'll tell you my secret first." His voice held a smile.

"Is it the good or the bad thing?" she asked.

"I'm twenty-six years old and would you believe my grandmother still has the ability to scare me? I'm dreading my grandparents coming home." Sebastian stopped walking and sighed as he looked out over the river. Tiny splashes rippled the water in the moonlight and he had his camera up and focused without even being aware he'd dropped Isabella's hand. "I don't want to sound like a whinger, but my family has this thing about me being lucky. It was even my nickname for a while before I lost my cool a few years back."

"Why lucky?" Isabella leaned against the trunk of a tree that was between them and the water.

"They reckon everything I touch goes my way, and things fall in my lap. I know I'm laid-back, but they don't need me carrying on about how hard I've worked to get where I am. So they just see it as 'oh lucky, Seb, he's fallen on his feet again.'"

"Having a work ethic and *telling* everyone how hard you work are two different things. Dad's a bit the same with me," she said softly. "Not so much doubting that I work hard but understanding that I need to. He can't see why I have to work so hard to get where I want to be."

"Why do you?" Sebastian wondered if he'd got too personal when she didn't answer for a while.

"I guess it's because I'm scared of failing. Lots of deep-seated family reasons there, but I won't go into them. Just rest assured that I totally understand what you're saying about family."

"I guess I sound like a real whiner, but—"

"No, not at all. I appreciate that you trust me enough to tell me how you feel."

"Ditto."

"Okay, that's the deep and meaningful ticked off for the night. Now let me tell you why I wanted to come out here tonight. I have a proposition for you."

"Ooh, is my reputation about to be compromised?" Isabella looked around. "I guess there's no one here to see, anyway."

Chapter Nine

Isabella wished she'd had Sebastian's camera in her hand to capture the priceless look on his face. The light was brighter now that the moon had risen higher, and even though his face was all planes and shadows and angles, his mouth dropped open and his eyes widened. Isabella had made that provocative statement on purpose; the conversation had been way too intense.

She giggled. "Don't worry. I'm not going to jump your bones in the middle of a paddock. And besides, I'll have you know, that when I did jump on you at the airport, that was way out of character. I'm really very quiet and shy."

"I don't believe that," he said, but he laughed, too. "Bella, you can jump my bones whenever you want."

The diminutive of her name sounded sweet in his deep and sexy voice but she demurred. "Not usually until after the second date," she said with a grin. "And so far, we've only had one." She tipped her head to the side. "And that probably doesn't count because your family was there."

"Okay, so tell me what counts as a date so I know how to

be prepared." A devilish light glinted in his eyes as he smiled.

She put a finger to her lips and pretended to be serious, enjoying the banter between them. "*Hmm*, let me see. Roses, definitely roses. Lots of roses. And definitely champagne. A huge bottle. Oh and candles are a must."

He shook his head, and his deep laugh rang out through the still night. "Okay, so I guess the dinner at the RSL doesn't even count as a date."

"No, I guess it wasn't."

"So the pressure's on." His laugh was wicked but enticing. "I'll have to start from scratch."

His laugh kept the smile on her face. "So now we have the date bit and bone-jumping prerequisites sorted, tell me about your real proposition."

"It's pretty exciting. For me, at least." Sebastian held out his hand again. "Come and we'll find somewhere to sit, and I'll tell you all about it."

She took his hand, and her fingers tingled when he laced his fingers through hers as he led her to the riverbank. A grassy spot levelled out where the water came into a tiny bay.

"Do you want to sit on my coat?" He let go of her hand and began to take his leather jacket off.

"No, it's fine. The grass is dry. And it's a bit nippy for you to sit there in a T-shirt." Not that she would have minded the view of muscled arms but, if all was said and done, he looked just as sexy in the leather jacket.

Isabella sat down carefully—not too close to Sebastian, but near enough to be able to hear what he was saying.

"I've been offered a photographic contract," he said.

She stared at him. That was the last thing she'd expected him to say. "I thought you were committed to the farm?" She tipped her head to the side and watched as he leaned closer.

"I am. But this way it's like having the best of both worlds. I can do it from here, from the farm, I mean. At nights and weekends. I'm going to tell Liam I won't work weekends."

"But on a farm don't some things have to be done every day?" She shook her head. "I don't know. Like feeding cattle or something."

He laughed. "Cattle eat grass and feed themselves. But there are some chores that have to be done. I'll have to cut a deal with Liam. A trade off." Sebastian picked up a flat stone and threw it onto the still water of the river. It jumped three times.

"Will there be a problem?" she asked.

The smile had gone from his face. "Liam will see it as another lucky break for me. He'll say, 'So wonder boy has a choice photographic contract drop into his lap and expects everyone to take up the slack and work for him.'"

"Do you really need to do it?"

"You mean do I need the money?"

A flush heated Isabella's neck and ran up into her cheeks. She was pleased it was dark. "No, that's not what I meant. I mean if it's going to cause trouble between you and your cousin, and there's work to be done at the farm on weekends, do you really need to take it on?"

"Yes, taking photos is as natural to me as breathing. It's something I need to do." This time when he threw the stone at the water, it was with a lot more force and it sank without skipping. "And to be honest, it's a means of getting away on the weekends once Gran and Pop come home. I don't fancy being stuck at the farm all the time. I know they've handed the farm over to the four of us, but the farmhouse is still their home. It's not home for me. I'm used to being independent." He stopped talking and stared at her. "Hey, I didn't mean to dump all that on you."

"Hey, I dumped my family stuff on you. I'm happy to listen."

"Thank you. We're a good pair. I'll miss having someone

to dump on when you go to England." Sebastian grinned.

"There's always email," she said.

"That would be nice."

"Now what's this job you mentioned before we got serious?"

"It's an easy one, and it could be fun. If I'm going out in the wilds on weekends with my camera, I need a photographic assistant. How would you like to help me out?"

. . .

After he'd dropped Isabella back in town, Sebastian rode home with a smile on his face. She'd agreed to come out and help him when he went away for the weekends, as long as she had enough time to get the catering organised. They probably wouldn't get a chance to go out till the wedding was over, but at least he'd see her when she was at the farm working on that. There were a couple of other reasons that made delaying the shoots more attractive. He could take his time telling Liam about the contract and work extra hard to help him get up-to-date with the farm work, and it also gave him more time to research some tips on night photography. It was a new area for him, and one he was excited about.

In the end, they'd agreed to go out the weekend after next.

The cattle grate rattled beneath the bike as he turned onto the driveway to the farmhouse, and he realised he was a lot more excited about learning how to take night photos than learning about the wheat harvest or how to fatten cattle.

But most of all, he was looking forward to going bush with Isabella. The next couple of months were going to be busy, but it was going to be fun.

What bothered him was the time after Isabella left to go to her new job, and he'd fulfilled the photography contract.

He could see the years ahead on the farm stretching in front of him, and that prospect didn't appeal at all. It was too far to get on his bike and head to the city every weekend. By the time he got there, it'd be time to turn around and come home again.

Sebastian put his motorbike away in the shed, checked on Daisy and the pups, and then headed for the house. He'd enjoyed the time with Isabella by the river. She made him laugh with her sense of humour.

As he walked into the kitchen, the flashing light on the answering machine next to the phone caught his attention. He pressed the play button and the robotic voice told him, there was one new message.

"Sebastian. It's Gran. We're on our way home. I tried to call Liam but he didn't answer. Come to Narrabri Airport tomorrow at lunchtime to collect us. Please."

Sebastian tried not to roll his eyes. At least she'd added a "please" to the royal command. He walked across to the large kitchen window that overlooked the paddocks.

The thought of living in a house with his grandparents was not one that sat comfortably with him.

I wonder if I could find a nice block of land out there and build my own place?

He shivered. That seemed way too permanent.

Chapter Ten

Sebastian was still in his boxers and drinking his second coffee when Liam arrived on horseback just after light the next morning. He'd slept well, but he'd had crazy dreams about Isabella. They'd been taking photographs together in Italy, but he'd lost her in a vineyard and had spent most of the dream trying to find her. Rose bushes with gigantic blooms had kept snagging him and he couldn't find her. He'd slept through the first alarm and woken with a start when the wind had sent something crashing against the side of the house.

"Enough left in the pot for me?" Liam asked with a wide yawn as he came through the back door.

"Sure. Help yourself, I'll go and get dressed."

"We'll be on horseback most of the day, and that wind's cold. It's turned to the south, so you'll need a jacket."

"Yeah, I heard it hit about an hour ago." Sebastian crossed to the window. Grey heavy clouds were building from the south, forecasting a wet and cold day.

He grimaced.

Yuk. A wet day on horseback.

Not his first choice for a way to spend a day.

"Won't be all day for one of us," he said hopefully.

"Why, what else is on?" Liam looked up from pouring his coffee.

"Gran rang last night. They're flying in to Narrabri at lunchtime and want to be collected."

"Do you want to go?" Liam's look was intense. "Or would you rather I did?"

Sebastian shrugged, not wanting Liam to think he wasn't up to spending the day working. What he would have preferred was to boot up his laptop, load the pictures he took last night, and layer some of the raw images. "We could both go. You wanted to look for those tractor parts, didn't you? Probably more chance of getting them in Narrabri than in town here."

"Yeah, that makes sense." Liam carried his coffee over to the table and pulled out a chair. "Get your skates on because I want to cut out the cattle in the back paddock. We should just have time before we go."

"Yes, sir." Sebastian shot him a grin and headed for the bathroom. A quick shower would wake him up.

Old Sam was Sebastian's favourite mount; the old white horse whickered a welcome as they walked across to the horse paddock, and Sebastian took a deep breath of the fresh country air as he stroked his nose.

"Did you miss me, Sam?"

It wasn't so bad once they were out in the paddocks and the cattle were cooperative. The rain held off, and once they started work, Sebastian shed his coat.

After the cattle were secured in the new paddock, they rode the eastern boundary fence together. Liam had noticed some cattle from the property next door on their land the other day and wanted to find where they'd broken through the fence.

"That old bloke Ferguson does nothing to keep the fences in good order. Pop's been complaining about him since we were kids." Liam shook his head.

"I remember that." Sebastian looked around. They were on a slight rise and could see to the horizon in all directions. "Now that Jemima's over at Daniela, and Lucy's with Garth at the McKenzie farm, most of the land we can see is part of the family holding, apart from the Ferguson farm."

"Yeah." Liam pulled his horse to a stop. "I want to talk to you about that. I reckon we should make Ferguson an offer for his place. He's got no kids, and he's getting a bit long in the tooth to be worrying about a property that size. He hasn't had a wheat crop in for the last few years, and it's prime land."

Sebastian swivelled around in the saddle. "How are we going to afford that?"

"We could do it with a loan. Do you have a problem with us expanding?"

"Haven't we got more land now than we can handle?" He bit his tongue before he could add that there were only so many working days in a week.

"It's manageable and the extra land to plant wheat would double our income in five years or so. The loan wouldn't be an issue."

Five years. Will I still be here doing this every day in five years? A heavy feeling settled in Sebastian's gut, but he didn't say anything.

"Sounds like something we should give serious thought to," he said, injecting enthusiasm that he didn't feel into his voice. "Let's sit down with Pop and see what he thinks once they've been home a few days." Maybe he hadn't put quite enough enthusiasm into his tone because Liam shot him a curious look.

"If we do go ahead, it'll mean working seven days a week until we get the harvest over. You up for that?"

"This year's harvest?" Sebastian settled a bit; that wouldn't be too bad.

"No, the first harvest from any wheat we plant on Ferguson's place, if we do buy it. It'll be a year or two before we harvest over there."

The heavy feeling in Sebastian's stomach solidified into a rock. "Okay. We'll talk about it with Pop."

They didn't speak again until they were almost to the house paddock, and Sebastian reined in his horse.

"Oh damn. Will you look at that!"

Liam pulled up his horse beside him. "I know. It's about time we got it fixed. But until the feed prices come down, we'll just have to put up with it."

Sebastian looked at him with a frown. "Put up with what?"

"The old pump. What were you looking at?" Liam put his hand up to his eyes and squinted. The sun was bright and reflecting off the iron roof of the hayshed.

Sebastian nudged old Sam and he took off at a canter as the lush house paddock came into sight.

"Yeah, the pump. Shame about that," he said to Liam when he caught up to them.

Sebastian was quiet as they took care of the horses. He hadn't even noticed the damn pump. If he'd told Liam he was looking at the rainbow that had framed the wheat perfectly as it arced above the irrigation spray, and cursing that he wasn't holding his camera, he knew he would have gotten a disgusted look.

He bit back the sigh that threatened as they headed back to the house for smoko.

. . .

Isabella woke up, determined to put a bright spin on the day, no matter what her father said. Nothing had changed with her dad, and nothing would change, unless she could convince him to sell or shut up shop and go back to Mum in Italy. At least last night had been fun and being with Sebastian had lightened her mood.

She pulled on a pair of jeans and a T-shirt and wandered down the stairs. A busy day stretched ahead: finalising the menu for the wedding, and making calls to suppliers, although both Angie and Jemima had asked her to source as much as possible from the local IGA supermarket.

"Too many businesses are closing; we need to shop local as much as we can," Jemima had said.

"Yes, I noticed the street had changed a lot since we left school. I don't know how Dad keeps the milk bar running."

As she pushed open the plastic strips that divided the back of the kitchen to the stairway, the buzz of conversation met her.

"Good girl," her father said with a huge grin as he rang up a sale. "I was about to call you. Shirley and I can't keep up."

Isabella widened her eyes. The crowd waiting to be served at the counter was three deep, and every table inside the café was full. She stood on her toes and looked over the crowded café. The tables outside were all occupied, too.

She rolled up her long-sleeved T-shirt. "Okay, tell me what to do."

"Do you remember how to work the coffee machine?'

"I do."

"Thanks, sweetheart, make a start there. There's about ten orders backed up."

Isabella shook her head, surprised at how busy the milk

bar was. The first few coffees were collected by Shirley, the waitress, and then when they caught up, Isabella delivered them to the tables.

"Are you Con's daughter?" an older lady asked as she placed the coffee on the table.

"I am."

"I could tell," she said. "You look like your father. He's a fine-looking man."

Isabella bit back a giggle.

Maybe once, but there isn't much of a resemblance between us these days. Dad was bald, and his tummy was quite large. She watched as Dad talked to the patrons at the tables. His voice boomed out, his eyes bright as he turned on the charm and had the group of elderly ladies at the back hanging off his every word.

An hour later, the last group walked out and Isabella drew a breath. "How often does that happen?"

"Not as often as I'd like," Dad said as he filled the sink with hot water. "It was the annual general meeting of the CWA."

"Ah, so a one-off."

"At least I knew they were coming, and Shirley cooked up a few cakes for us, didn't you, Shirl?" He looked around with a shrug. "Where did she go?"

"Last I saw she was heading for the back alley with a cigarette."

Her father shook his head. "Thanks for the help anyway. It's a shame—"

"No Dad. Don't start. I'm in a good mood. I was happy to help out, but now I've got a lot to do. I've picked up a second job for while I'm here so I have to get this wedding organised."

"Another job? I won't see you if you work too much. What's this second job?"

"I'll be helping Sebastian with a photo shoot."

Isabella refused to let the look of crafty satisfaction on his face get to her. If Dad wanted to think she might hang around here and not go to England because she'd fall for a local guy, and use her to make coffee in the milk bar when he was busy, that was his problem, not hers. She wasn't going to let it put her in a bad mood again.

But it's hard.

She headed back upstairs and picked up her to-do list for the day. Biting her lip, she looked at her phone sitting next to the computer, and before she could change her mind, she picked it up and hit speed dial.

He answered immediately. "Bella, hi. What are you up to?"

"Hi Sebastian, can I arrange a time to come out and have another look at the kitchen and ovens at the farm?"

"Sure."

"When would suit you best?" Isabella twirled her hair around her finger as she waited for his reply.

"Listen, why don't you come tonight? We're having a bit of a get-together. Just the family. And everyone will be here to answer any questions you might have about the wedding."

"Um. Are you sure that would be okay?"

"It'll be perfect."

"Okay as long as you're sure. What time and what can I bring?"

"About six thirty." The laughter in his voice was clear. "Roses and champagne?"

Isabella smiled but she injected a prim tone into her voice. "This is a working visit, not a date."

"Damn, I thought it was worth a try."

"You're mad, you know that?"

"So they tell me. And hey, thanks for the company last night." His voice was soft. "I really enjoyed myself."

"Me, too," she said.

"Bella?" She loved the deep husky tone when he lowered his voice.

"Bring your dad with you. Gran and Pop are home. Maybe he'd like a night out, too."

"Thank you. I'll bring my specialty, too."

As Isabella set off to the IGA store with her menu and list, she still had a smile on her face.

Chapter Eleven

The trip to Narrabri had been successful. They'd come home with the tractor parts, Gran and Pop, and a load of luggage.

"I swear we buy a new suitcase in every city we visit." Pop had shaken his head as Liam and Sebastian squeezed the four large suitcases into the boot at the airport.

Everyone was at the farm, and the welcome-home celebration was in full swing.

"Well, we're home for a while now, so you don't have to worry." Gran's smile was satisfied. She patted Sebastian's shoulder as she walked back into the house. "Thanks for getting us today, love."

Sebastian stayed out on the verandah with Garth and Liam. Liam had tried to talk farm with Pop but Pop put up his hand, much to Sebastian's relief.

"No, Liam, we'll do that in the office tomorrow. This is a party." Pop lifted his beer and took a swig. "There is nothing in the world that beats a good cold Aussie beer."

Gran came back out of the kitchen wiping her hands on her apron. It was as though she'd never been away. "Don't you go drinking too much beer, Harry Peterkin."

She looked at Sebastian and winked. "You make sure your grandfather behaves, won't you, Seb? He overdid it in the German beer halls, and I almost had to carry him back to the hotel myself."

"That, I'd like to see," Liam said with a chuckle.

"And who's going to make sure I behave?" Sebastian asked, sharing a conspiratorial look with Pop. There hadn't been a cross word since Gran had got off the plane at lunchtime and hugged him close.

Maybe she truly was happy now that he was back at the farm.

Maybe I've grown up a bit, too. Learned a bit of patience and tolerance since I was last here.

"Isabella will," Liam said, nudging Sebastian with his shoulder. "I think our Seb's a bit smitten by the Italian beauty."

"Isabella? Is that the girl who's helping out at the wedding?" Gran asked. "Con's daughter?"

"Yes, she's coming over in a while. I thought it would be nice for you to meet her, seeing as she'll be taking over the kitchen in a couple of weeks. I invited Con, too."

Gran and Liam shared a smile.

"Here's Bella!" Ned and Jemima's Gwennie ran down the steps and waited until the bright yellow Citroën was parked before she ran over to open the door.

"Bella's won quite a few hearts out here already," Liam said drily.

Sebastian put his beer down on the table and headed towards the steps. Even though Gran lowered her voice, he still heard every word clearly.

"Maybe that's what our Seb needs. A love interest to convince him to stay here."

He clenched his hands as he walked down the steps.

That'd be right. Gran didn't think he had the staying power unless there was an enticement.

Nothing has changed.

• • •

"Do you want me to help you get the things out of the boot?" her father asked as he climbed out of the driver's side. The trip from town had been interesting, to say the least. Isabella's legs were still like jelly. Dad had overtaken cattle trucks and semitrailers without a care in the world.

It's a wonder we're still alive.

"No, I'll get them. You go over and say hello." She walked around to the back of the car and opened the boot. "And I'll drive home so you can have a wine or two." She grinned back at him as he gave her the thumbs-up. He'd been like a kid at Christmas since she'd passed on Sebastian's invitation.

"Wonderful. I haven't see Harry and Helena for a couple of years." He headed off towards the group sitting on the verandah while Isabella got the carry bag from the boot.

"Let me take that for you." Sebastian reached over for the insulated bag, and she handed it to him.

"What is that incredible smell?" he asked.

"Just a little something I brought along for dinner." Isabella smiled when he inhaled and closed his eyes.

"That aroma takes me right back to Italy." He grinned at her and her heart did a funny little flip. "Gran believes in wholesome country cooking. The only herbs she uses come from a jar." He sniffed again. "I can smell real garlic, oregano, and—"

"And fresh tomatoes. Dad has a lovely little garden behind the café. Wait there and I'll get the roses from the back seat."

"Roses?" His mouth fell open. "You brought roses?"

"Didn't you ask for champagne and roses?" She threw him a cheeky grin. Keeping him on his toes was fun. "The champagne's in the bag."

"Where the heck did you find fresh roses in Spring Downs?"

"It was hard but where there's a will there's a way." She wasn't going to tell him that the idea had come to her when she'd been in the IGA and the delivery of fresh fruit and vegetables—and flowers—had come while she was talking to the order clerk. "And don't get your hopes up, boyo, they're not for you. They're for your grandmother, as a thank you for having us both visit."

She laughed when he put on a pretend pout. "And what do I get?"

"You get the pleasure of my company."

"So still not a date?"

"Nope."

Once she'd taken the roses from the car, Isabella put her arm through Sebastian's and they walked across the lawn together.

"Gran. Do you remember Isabella? Bella, this is my grandmother, Helena." Sebastian introduced her when they reached the verandah.

Isabella was surprised. Considering Helena had grown-up grandchildren, she looked younger than she'd expected. She was tall and slim, with fair skin and blonde hair pulled back into a braid.

Helena held out her hand. Her skin was soft, and her perfume was a modern one that Isabella recognised.

"Welcome, Isabella. And I'm sorry I don't remember you, but I did work with your mother on the CWA. She was a wonderful cook, and we used her skills mercilessly. We should get you to join us."

"Oh, I'm only here for a visit, Helena. Although I did

meet quite a few of the CWA ladies in the milk bar yesterday."

"Oh, I thought you'd moved back to live with your dad."

"Oh no. I'm just here for a visit." Isabella was taken aback by the glance that Helena shot at Sebastian. It contained disappointment and something else she couldn't put her finger on.

Helena took the bag from him. "Oh thank you, Isabella. You didn't need to bring anything."

"I thought I'd do a sample of one of the dishes I'm considering for the wedding. Then you can all tell me if it suits what you have in mind."

"It smells wonderful, and it's lovely to have you here. Come on in. The girls are out the back talking weddings." She put her arm around Isabella's shoulder as they walked onto the verandah. "Seb, you can bring this in, pour us a drink, and then come join us."

"Yes, Gran." He caught Isabella's eye and grinned.

Lucy, Angie, and Jemima were at a large table poring over a magazine.

"Oh, you're here, Isabella. Look what we found!" Excitement filled Lucy's voice.

"Gran bought the magazine at the London airport," Jemima explained.

Isabella crossed to the table and looked down at the glossy magazine. It was a double-page spread of photographs and an article on the top restaurants of England. Lucy pointed to the picture in the bottom right corner. "Look, it's your restaurant. The Three Ducks!"

"Your restaurant?" Helena stared at her. "How can it be your restaurant?" Her brow was wrinkled in a frown.

Isabella laughed. "It's not my restaurant, but when I leave here I'm going to work there as a *sou*s chef."

"Well, how special is that! Harry and I had dinner there the week before last."

"What a coincidence!" Angie exclaimed.

Lucy looked at Jemima and then at Gran. "It's not the one you were telling us about before you left, was it, Gran? The one that's near where you grew up."

Helena's eyes sparkled. "It is, and when we went to look at the old house we decided to stay in town and have dinner there. It's an absolutely beautiful place, and the food was divine."

"The old house?" Isabella asked.

"Gran grew up in London," Lucy explained. "Notting Hill. Just like the movie that Julia Roberts was in. But her family had a country estate near Windsor Castle."

"I loved that movie. And I didn't know that you were from London, Helena!" Angie exclaimed. "Liam never mentioned it."

"So how did you get to Spring Downs?" Isabella asked. "It's a long way from London."

"I love the story." Lucy jumped in. "It's a lesson for all of us, if only we'd known it when we were wondering whether to come home." She put her hand on her heart and fluttered her eyelids, much to the amusement of the others. "True love!"

"So tell us, please? We want to know. There's nothing like a real-life romance." Angie looked at Isabella and she nodded.

"Gran and Pop met on a kibbutz in Israel." Lucy looked at Helena who had a dreamy look on her face. "Harry, was a fine strapping young man, a young Australian farm boy from Western New South Wales, and Helena was the pretty social butterfly from Notting Hill in London." Lucy put her hand on her heart. "They fell in love at first sight."

"We did." Helena smiled at Lucy. "How many times did you sit at my knee and listen to this story, Lucy?"

"Oh, dozens. But I still see the way Pop looks at you, and it makes me all warm and gooey inside. I always said I wouldn't marry until I found a man who looked at me like that."

"And you found one in your own backyard." Helena pulled Lucy in for a hug. "I've missed you grandchildren while we've travelled the world."

"And we missed you, too. And I did find Garth, even though I couldn't see what was in front of me until we went through all sorts of angst."

"I missed Harry so much, when he went home to Australia I followed him to see this Pilliga Scrub he went on about." Helena added for Isabella and Angie's benefit. "And I fell in love with the land, too."

"That's a beautiful story." Isabella swallowed down the ache in her throat. "It's not often that you hear about a love match like that. But I'm a career girl, and it will be a long time before I'm looking for a soul mate."

Helena smiled and nodded. "You often don't have the chance to choose when love finds you."

"Cupid and all that," Lucy added. And to add to the mushy atmosphere, Angie sniffed a tear back.

Discomfort filled Isabella. All this emotion was a bit too up close and personal for her. She felt like she'd walked into the Hallmark channel. She rubbed her hands together. "Okay, let's go back to the kitchen, and you can show me the ovens."

Jemima waved an elegant hand from her chair.

"You don't need me there," Jemima said. "I don't know one end of the oven from another."

"Maybe, Isabella can give you some cooking lessons while she's here." Helena's voice was dry. "Sometimes I worry about Ned and those poor children." She turned to Isabella. "Jemima is more interested in her horses than learning how to cook."

"I'm doing okay." Jemima's voice held amusement. "No

one's starved yet."

Angie and Lucy followed Helena and Isabella as they went back to the kitchen.

"The preparation space looks adequate," Isabella said briskly. As she glanced over at the benchtops, she was surprised to see Sebastian in the doorway, his expression intense.

"Great, here's Seb with our drinks." Helena waved him in.

Once the drinks were passed around, he didn't stay. Lucy took Isabella on a tour of the whole kitchen area. The walk-in pantry, the laundry with its huge chest freezers, and the old concrete tubs in the corner of the back verandah were all discussed for the wedding reception.

"We can fill these with ice and keep a lot of the salad stuff cool on the morning of the wedding," Helena said, but Isabella was only half paying attention, wondering why Sebastian had taken off so quickly.

"It all looks perfect," Isabella said with a nod. "It's almost as good as a commercial kitchen."

"When we have the harvesters here, we have to feed a couple of dozen workers at a time. We took that into account when we redid the house a few years ago."

"Come on, that's enough work. Let's go back out in the cool breeze," Lucy said. "I'm sure you'll have no problem finding everything."

"And you'll have plenty of help, too," Helena said.

Isabella walked behind Lucy and her grandmother as they stepped out onto the verandah.

"So what do you think of Seb coming home, Gran?" Lucy's voice was quiet, and Isabella paused to let them have a private conversation.

Gran's reply was quiet, but Isabella caught it. "That boy won't stay here, but he has to realise that for himself."

Isabella was thoughtful as she walked to the table and sat down beside Jemima. It sounded as though Sebastian really was the odd one out in the family. She shrugged; she felt sorry for him, but she had enough problems of her own with Mum and Dad. She wasn't going to get involved in another family's issues.

There was no such thing as a perfect family. She'd learned that firsthand.

Chapter Twelve

The intense atmosphere lightened considerably when they all sat around the dinner table, and it was easier for Isabella to believe in happy families again. The pasta sauce she'd made had been a hit, and even the children had asked for more. They were excited, and after they'd finished eating, Sebastian egged the two girls on, much to Jemima's displeasure.

"Don't encourage them, Seb. You're as bad as they are."

He was showing them how to balance a spoon on their noses, and they were in awe when it fell off his nose three times in a row. Isabella couldn't keep a straight face.

Ryan tugged at Sebastian's jeans, and they shared a look. A minute later they had both disappeared under the table.

Helena rolled her eyes as she bounced baby James on her knee. "Honestly, Harry, that boy will never grow up. He reminds me of you more and more every day."

Harry and Isabella's father were discussing the football at full volume, and Harry turned to his wife one hand cupped to his ear. "What did you say, love?"

"Never mind." She waved her hand. "Go back to your

football."

Isabella sat back and let the happy noise wash around her. For the first time since she'd arrived in Spring Downs, the empty feeling of being in an unfamiliar environment disappeared.

Something tickled her leg and, lifting the tablecloth, she peeked under the table. She smiled as she spotted the little brown spaniel that Liam usually had nipping at his heels. He looked up at her and licked her foot.

Next minute, a pair of brown eyes, and a younger pair of blue eyes peered at her. "I hope you didn't think that was us," Sebastian said with a grin.

"I think Ryan has much better manners than that," she replied.

"What about me?" Sebastian asked in a mock hurt tone.

"I'm not so convinced about your manners. The spoon on the nose during dessert has made me wonder."

"It was a clean spoon," he protested. "It didn't have any custard on it."

"Just as well." Isabella giggled. "You're quite mad, you know."

Ryan ran off to play with the girls when Ned told them they could leave the table; Sebastian crawled out and sat beside her in the chair that Kelsey had vacated.

"Having a good time?" he asked.

"I am. What about you?"

"You need to ask that? I love kids," he said.

"You are still a big kid," Liam said from across the table. "I doubt if Seb will ever grow up," he added for Isabella's benefit.

"And I'm happy like that," Sebastian said, picking up the spoon again and tipping his head back.

"No." A chorus of groans sounded.

"You will make a great father," said her father, and

Isabella tensed as he looked at her with a calculating glint in his eye. She glared at him, willing him not to say anything more but he ignored her. "I am so looking forward to having my own grandchildren running around like this one day. It will be wonderful." He put his hand on his chest and let out such a loud sigh, Isabella was hard pressed not to pick up her spoon and bop him on the nose.

Sebastian reached over and squeezed her hand sympathetically as silence descended around the table. Unfortunately, his grandmother leaned forward and saw him take her hand, and she nudged Harry.

"It will be." Isabella decided it was easier not to react. "Now let's get these dishes done and I can see how this kitchen work space flows. Lucy and Angie said that the helpers will be from the CWA, Helena?" She pulled her hand out of Sebastian's warm clasp. Altogether too many people were jumping to the wrong conclusion.

They were not a couple. And wouldn't be, ever.

She glanced down at him as she stood and began to clear the table.

Sebastian was like a forbidden dessert. If she was honest with herself, she knew she was tempted, but he would be bad for her in so many ways.

She was only here for a few weeks—he was here to stay. Besides, he was too lightweight for her tastes. She preferred a man who— A man who what?

Maybe someone who had a stronger work ethic? Maybe someone a little bit more serious about life?

One who was more serious about setting a goal and working hard to achieve it?

When she found a partner—or a soul mate—it would be someone who had a work ethic that matched hers. It was all very well to talk about love at first sight, but life didn't work like that. You had to share common interests and be similar in what you wanted out of life to make a relationship work.

Her life goals were set, and she was on her way to achieve them. Isabella wasn't sure if Sebastian even knew what he wanted.

But in the scheme of things, that didn't matter because once she went to England, she would probably never see him again.

Why did that make her feel so sad?

• • •

Sebastian could pinpoint the exact second that Isabella judged him and he was found wanting. A spark of temper sizzled for a second, and then he shrugged it off. He didn't care what people thought about him.

He knew what he wanted out of life, but he also knew he had to do the right thing by his family. If they were two different things, so be it. He would do what was right and what was expected, but he wasn't prepared to take the judgment that came along with it. Luckily, no one picked up on his mood, and he managed to join in on the laughing conversation as it turned to the wedding.

"As well as being my best man, Sebastian is going to take the photographs, Gran," Liam said after the girls had cleared the table. Pop was in there helping them wash up.

"So you brought your cameras and gear with you?" Gran asked. "That was thoughtful of you."

He stayed calm.

Thoughtful!

"Yes. I had all my gear sent from the airport by a courier. You obviously haven't been in the spare room yet, Gran. It's full of my stuff, and I've got my computer set up there. If it's in the way, just let me know."

And I'll move out. Find a place to rent. But it wasn't

the right time to say that. It was already starting to feel claustrophobic being in the house with Gran and Pop. As much as he loved them, he hadn't planned on living in a house with a couple in their seventies.

And they'd been home less than a day.

"Tell me about your photography, Sebastian. Bella tells me you took photos in Italy." Con's voice broke into his musing.

"Yes, I was working with the *Firenze* tourist agency."

Con nodded. "And now you have work here, too, and my Bella is going to help you with a photo shoot?"

Damn, I didn't want that out yet.

"What photo shoot?" Liam stared at him.

"Don't worry, it's only nights and weekends." Sebastian waved a casual hand. "It's just a contract taking a few shots of stars." He played it down before Liam started in on him. "I was going to tell you about it later."

"Photos of the stars? Now that sounds romantic," Gran said.

"Yes, I'm doing an Outback series." He turned to his grandmother. "Don't worry, it's only a weekend thing. It won't take away from me working on the property. Not one bit."

"I wasn't worried," she said. "It's always good to have other interests. Liam and Garth have the alliance. Ned has the children, and all of their activities."

Ned laughed. "It sure keeps me busy. Did I tell you that Ryan scored his first goal in the under-fives at soccer last weekend?"

Sebastian relaxed as the focus of the conversation moved away from him as everyone congratulated Ryan, and then the conversation moved to the races next weekend.

"Are you coming to the CBC races, Isabella?" Gran asked.

"CBC?"

"Come-by-Chance. It's a tiny town about thirty kilometres down our road. The racecourse is on one of the cattle properties."

She shook her head. "I don't know. I saw the sign about the races when we were out the other night, but I hadn't really thought about going."

Everyone spoke at once. "You have to come."

"It's the social event of the season."

Her father looked at Isabella. "Of course we'll be there. I wouldn't miss it for the world."

Isabella looked up and her gaze connected with Sebastian's as she smiled. "Okay, I guess I'll be there then."

Sebastian stood and crossed to the verandah railing and looked out over the paddocks. It was a clear night, and the array of stars lit up the night sky. His fingers itched to hold his camera.

What Gran didn't know was that the *farm* was his other interest. His photography was his heart and soul.

But he wasn't going to set that cat amongst the pigeons.

Chapter Thirteen

Isabella had hoped that her father would snooze on the way back to town.

But, of course, she had no such luck.

She slowed the car at the intersection where the road that led down to the farm met the Pilliga Forest Way. She wondered about going to the races.

It was great to have company and have some social functions to go to—the family and all the kids were great fun—but it brought her in Sebastian's company often, and she wasn't sure how she felt about that.

Her head told her what she should be doing, but her heart said, "Spend the time with him while you're here. Life isn't all about work."

Live life, Isabella.

It was as though her father read her thoughts, and she jumped as he spoke.

"They certainly live a good life out on their farms, don't they, *cara*?"

She gripped the steering wheel tightly, knowing she was

stuck with Dad and his conversation for the next half hour. If Dad wanted to have his say, he would. She racked her mind trying to think of a way to divert him. She was having enough trouble sorting her own thoughts without him throwing in his bit.

"You know, if you went back to Italy, you'd be close to your family," she said. Dad had a couple of brothers and a sister in Tuscany.

There! She'd thrown down the gauntlet. He didn't answer.

"And Mum works hard over there," she said. "I think she does it to have some company."

"I send her plenty of money. She doesn't need to work." Dad folded his arms and didn't speak for a moment. Guilt rippled through Isabella, and she softened her approach.

"I do worry about you, Dad. Can I ask you something?"

He shot her a sideways glance. "What?"

"Do you miss Mum?"

"Of course, I miss your mother. She is the love of my life."

Isabella shook her head. "So why won't you follow her?"

He shrugged. "Because she doesn't love me. If she did, she would have stayed with me."

Isabella knew she was close to being able to make a difference in two lives that were so important to her, but to do so she had to break a promise, and she thought long and hard before she said anything. Biting her lip, she stared ahead as the headlights outlined the gum trees, the bark of their trunks stark white in the bright light. A kangaroo stood unblinking on the side of the road, and she slowed down in case it jumped onto the road, but it turned away and bounded back through the scrubby bush.

Maybe she didn't agree with what Mum had done, but she could understand how her vibrant mother didn't want to live in the Outback of Australia. But neither of her parents was happy.

"She does, Dad." Isabella kept her voice soft. "She made me promise not to tell you, but she misses you so much. When I left to come here, she hugged me and cried and told me how much she loves you. But like you, she is too stubborn to budge." She softened her words with a laugh. "No wonder I'm so stubborn with parents like you pair. It's gone on for way too long."

There was a heavy silence from the passenger side of the car, and her father turned away from her to stare through the window into the darkness of the bush that was flashing past.

"Really, tell me what is there here for you in this town?" Isabella wasn't going to give up now that she'd breached Mum's trust. "A few friends playing darts at the local club? Your customers in a milk bar that seems to have fewer people coming in every day?" She was determined to make her father see reason. Her hands were tight on the steering wheel. "Dad, Mum misses you so much. She has only a few friends, and she won't go to visit your family because she thinks they'll judge her. She's as unhappy as I know you are. Please, Daddy, promise me you'll think about it?"

Isabella sniffed as her voice broke, and she wiped her eyes with the back of one hand. As she put it back on her lap, her father reached over and squeezed it.

His voice was gruff. "I'll think about it."

She smiled as she accelerated down the road, but the smile didn't last long.

"Now it's my turn," he said.

"Your turn, what?" she said suspiciously.

"I saw the sparks between you and Sebastian tonight. What's going on there?"

"Nothing," she said, indignation lacing her voice. "I barely know him. I have no idea what your imagination has conjured up, Dad. Most likely it's wishful thinking."

Chapter Fourteen

"Isabella, it's Lucy."

"Hi, Luce. What's happening?" Isabella crossed to the window with her phone to her ear and looked down at the street. Dad was closing up downstairs, and the town was deserted.

As usual.

"I'm going to Dubbo tomorrow to look for an outfit for the races next Saturday, and I wondered if you'd like to come with me."

To Isabella, it was like a life buoy. She was about to go under from the boredom that had increased day by day. She'd done most of the organising for the wedding but had been putting off another visit out to the farm until some of the table decorations arrived.

It had been more than a week since the welcome home barbeque for Sebastian's grandparents and everyone had been busy. Dad had been quiet, and he'd spent a lot of time on the computer in the spare room of the apartment. Isabella had been on the phone and online, ordering food and decorating items for the wedding, which was now less than three weeks away. Sebastian had called to chat a couple of times, but she hadn't seen him.

She was not only bored, but strangely, she was feeling neglected.

Isabella checked the oven as she listened to Lucy. Dad was late up and she had dinner warming. "I'm in. It'll be great to have a catch up with you. I can get some of the stuff for the wedding tables while we're there." She pointed to the oven as her father came in the door. "So a new outfit? Is this a dress-up affair? I thought it was a casual thing, a bush race?"

"Didn't you ever go to one when we were in high school?" Lucy asked.

"No, I don't remember going. It was a long time ago."

"We dress up to the nines, and the judges come around and pick the candidates for the Miss Come-by-Chance for the year."

"I love the name of the town."

Lucy laughed. "It's not a town. You think Spring Downs is small. Wait till you see Come-by-Chance! Anyway it was named after an old sheep station when the district began to get settled."

"So what time will we go tomorrow?"

"How early can you be ready?"

Isabella hung up the phone with a smile and turned to her father, who was serving up the lasagne she'd cooked. "I'm going to Dubbo with Lucy tomorrow."

"I'm pleased." He dug into this pocket and pulled out his wallet as she watched with a frown. He pulled out a wad of notes and held them out to her. "Buy yourself a pretty dress for the picnic races while you're there."

Isabella shook her head. "No need for that, Dad. I've got plenty of money."

He pulled a face. "I'm sure you have, but humour your

dear old father. I would like to buy you a pretty dress."

"I don't need one. It's just more to pack when I leave."

"But you have to have a dress to wear to the races. I'm getting dressed up in my good clothes." He looked at her jeans and T-shirt. "I haven't seen you in a dress since you've arrived. You have to wear a dress to the races."

"Okay," she said with a smile as he handed her the money. "I'll let you buy me a dress." She reached up and kissed his cheek. "Thanks, Dad."

· · ·

It was like being back in her teens again. Lucy left James with her grandmother and picked Isabella up in town just after eight. They laughed and joked most of the trip to Dubbo, and Isabella relaxed in the passenger seat of the modern SUV.

"Coffee, first," announced Lucy as she pulled into a vacant space in the car park in the centre of town. "Although, I suppose coffee in Dubbo doesn't quite measure up to an Italian square," she said with a sigh. "One day when the children are old enough, Garth and I will travel."

"Children?" Isabella looked at Lucy curiously.

A strange feeling—almost envy—ran through Isabella as Lucy smiled and patted her flat tummy. "I think number two is on the way. He's announced his presence with another good dose of morning sickness. Garth's the only one who knows, so don't mention it in the presence of the family yet."

"I won't," Isabella said with a smile, pleased to be considered a close enough friend to hear the news first. "But congratulations, you must be excited."

"We are. And I'm looking forward to wearing a drop-dead gorgeous dress to the races before I get too big to dress fashionably again. With James, I wore almost-tents for the last month, I was so big. And he came early, so I hate to think how big I would have got if he'd arrived on his due date."

"Okay then, let's grab a coffee and hit the shops!" Isabella picked up her purse and opened the door before she turned to Lucy. "And just so you know, it's not the location that makes the coffee best, it's the company you have it with."

"I'm so going to miss you when you head off again." Lucy blew her a kiss and climbed from the car. "I suppose there's nothing that would make you change your mind?"

"No way! I'm so excited about this new job. When you and Garth travel, you'll have to come and visit me in England."

Their coffee break was full of chatter and laughter as Lucy caught Isabella up on everyone they'd gone to school with, before the conversation turned to Sebastian. She had a feeling that Lucy was probing, so she deliberately kept her responses flippant.

"I'm pleased that you and Seb have hooked up a bit. I worry about him out there on the farm with Gran and Pop," Lucy said as she put her cup back in the saucer. "He's a brilliant photographer, you know. I'm really surprised that he's come back out here to stay."

Isabella shrugged casually. "I'm sure he'll be able to do both. Work the farm and take his photos. I watched him working the other night. He's certainly got a passion for it."

"Has he said anything more to you, Bella? About staying out here? You seem to have struck up a friendship."

She replied slowly, taking care not to say anything that Sebastian maybe wouldn't want repeated to his family. "Not really. I think, like I said, he's keen to do both. Make a success of the farm and still do his photography."

Lucy frowned. "I really worry that his heart's not here at the farm, and that he's only staying to keep the family happy. You know, Gran's expectations and all that. She's a strong woman, but I know even Gran wonders if he'll stay. She was talking to me about it the other night."

"Maybe she needs to talk to *him* about it. He's a grown man, and I'm sure he'll do whatever's right for him, Luce." Isabella put her head to the side. "It might take him a month, it might take a couple of years, but whatever he's most passionate about will win in the end." Privately, she thought that Lucy was on the right track, but the Sebastian she'd gotten to know since she'd arrived was a man who would do the right thing by his family.

It bothered her. *If Sebastian can do the right thing, what does that say about me?*

"I know what you're saying though," she said. "I worry about Mum and Dad. Sebastian has obviously got family loyalty and wants to do the right thing by everyone. I'm the selfish one. I follow my path, and I leave Mum and Dad to worry about me."

Lucy reached over and touched her arm. "Oh Bella, don't be silly. Like Seb, you're a grown-up. You can't be responsible for everyone's happiness. You have to look out for yourself. One day when we don't have all this shopping to do, I'll tell you how I almost lost Garth by not following my heart."

"Thanks, I look forward to it. Now let's hit the shops."

Two hours later, they were standing together in the large department store in town. Lucy had been very persuasive, and Isabella shook her head at the bags that were lined up along the bench in the fitting room.

"I can't believe you talked me into all this. I'll never fit it all into my suitcase when I leave." She held up the pair of bright blue shoes she'd fallen in love with as soon as Lucy had picked them up. "Although, I will find room for the shoes."

"You have to get all dolled up for the Come-by-Chance races. It's the social event of the year for us. There'll be a few thousand people there."

"What? At the dirt racetrack that Sebastian took me past the other night? I saw the sign that said COME-BY-CHANCE RACE CLUB, but I thought it had closed down."

Lucy nodded with a smile. "Wait till you see it. It comes alive every year, and this year will be extra special. There's even silver trophies for the winners. That's why we have to get new clothes. I can't enter now because I'm married, but you'll have a good shot at the title."

Isabella frowned as she slipped the shoes back into the box. "What title?"

"Miss Come-by-Chance."

"On, no. Don't even think about entering me. I'm only here for a few more weeks. Besides, I don't agree with beauty contests."

"You don't enter. The judges walk around, and you'll get a tap on the shoulder." Lucy folded her arms and smiled. "It's only for the day, and it's a bit of fun. It's a tradition and sponsored by a local business. Come on, we've got to find us each a hat now."

Isabella shook her head and followed Lucy out of the change room, both laden with plastic shopping bags.

"I'm going to have a shot at Fashion of the Fields," Lucy added.

"Fashion of the Fields?" Isabella giggled.

"Yes. It's a hoot." Lucy tipped her head to the side as she tried on a black hat with a feather on the crown and a veil across her face.

"Gawd, Luce, you can't wear that. It looks like something you wear to a funeral." Isabella shook her head.

"The veil will keep the dust out of my mouth if it's windy. And we're getting you a hat, too."

"Sounds delightful. And"—she put her hands on her hips—"I'm not buying a hat."

"Oh yes you are." Lucy's smile was determined. "Come on, Bella, you'll have a great time."

"Maybe, but not with you wearing that hat." Isabella rolled her eyes as Lucy passed her a hat. Some battles weren't worth fighting.

"Okay, maybe not." Lucy squealed as Isabella put the hat on the side of her head. "Oh my God, look at that. It's perfect for you!"

And it had been. Isabella carried the bags into the small second bedroom above the milk bar that she'd turned into her home-away-from-home for the past few weeks. The trip to Dubbo had been a roaring success. New outfits for both of them—including hats, shoes, and handbags that Isabella didn't need.

It had been fun. She'd enjoyed every minute shopping with Lucy. It had been a long time since she'd treated herself to shopping and lunch with a girlfriend. Once she got to England, it would be all work again. So it was nice to enjoy the time here. She paused, deep in thought, as she went to put the hat carefully on the shelf in the wardrobe. It was easier for her to see now why Lucy enjoyed living out here. Lucy had a man who loved her, a gorgeous baby, and a house that Isabella had promised to visit.

"I have the best equipped kitchen. It's a shame the wedding's not at our place. Wait till you see my stove. I love baking." Lucy had prattled on as they'd walked from one end of the shopping plaza to the other. After they'd gone to the catering supplies warehouse, the back of Lucy's car had been loaded with decorations for the wedding reception— tablecloths, centrepieces, and heart-shaped chocolates wrapped in gold foil, and they both agreed it was more sensible that Lucy take it straight out to Prickle Creek Farm and store it for the wedding.

Isabella sat on the side of the bed, a little disappointed

that she hadn't gone out to the farm with Lucy, but it would have been too far for Lucy to drive her back, and following her out in Dad's old car, for no real reason other than unpacking a few boxes hadn't been worth the long drive. She unpacked the bags, hung the dress on a padded hanger, and put her shoes in the bottom of the old wooden wardrobe.

Dad was still down in the milk bar—she'd poked her head in the door to say she was back before she'd come upstairs. In the kitchen, she opened the fridge to see what she would cook for dinner and pulled out a can of soda water. She popped the top, poured it into a glass, and added some ice before she wandered over to the window and looked out at the street. It was just before closing time for all of the stores, but the main street was already deserted. A lone white ute chugged slowly down the centre of the road and disappeared around the corner. She could almost imagine tumbleweeds blowing down the street, adding to the mournful loneliness of the landscape. It seemed that all of the life in this region was out on the farms where life was interesting and social activities followed the working days.

Just over a month here, unless she could convince Dad to go to Italy before then. Isabella straightened her shoulders. Tonight she'd raise the subject carefully and see if she could persuade him. There was nothing here for Dad anymore, and he had a wife who loved and missed him over in Italy. There was nothing here for her, either.

Maybe, if he agreed, they could travel back together. With a determined nod of her head, she went back into the kitchen and made a start on dinner.

For some reason, she kept thinking about Sebastian. If she left early, she wouldn't be able to help him with his photo shoots.

Chapter Fifteen

Sebastian's mood wasn't good. The first he knew about Liam stocking the property with sheep was when Liam had taken him down to the back paddock in Pop's ute this morning. Liam had come over from his place on horseback because they were cutting cattle out later in the day.

Or that had been the plan.

Liam's plan, Sebastian thought crankily.

"So the sheep? Whose idea was that?" Sebastian pushed his hat back off his brow and stared at Liam.

"Pop suggested it." Liam slammed the ute door shut and glared at Sebastian. "Do you have a problem with that?"

"Maybe we could have discussed it, seeing I'm here now." He slammed the passenger door and strode around to the back of the ute where Liam was lifting out the wire to repair the fence.

"Here, take the wire strainers for me."

Sebastian walked over to the fence, tempted to say *take them yourself* but that would sound childish, and Liam would not hesitate to point that out.

Patience.

He'd been disappointed when Lucy had arrived late yesterday afternoon and asked him to unload the SUV with her and put the wedding decorations in Gran's spare room. Gran and Pop had gone to have dinner with their best friends, Ted and Julia, on the property up the road, and Sebastian was at a loose end.

Now that Lucy had brought the wedding stuff home that was one less visit Isabella would have to make out here. He'd been tempted to go into town, but apart from visiting her there'd been no reason to go. If he was honest, his black mood had started last night. In the end, he'd booted up his computer and manipulated those images he'd taken out at the old Paterson property the other night, and his mood had improved slightly.

One of the moonlit photographs was a stunner, and he put it in the folder ready to send off to Chris, and about midnight he'd walked quietly to the kitchen for a drink.

Gran and Pop had already gotten home and gone to bed. He'd picked up his phone from the kitchen bench, and his mood had plummeted again when he'd seen three missed calls from Isabella.

Damn, somehow the ring switch had been flipped to mute and he'd missed her calls. It was way too late to call her back now. She'd be in bed; an enticing image of Isabella's black curls spread out on a white pillow case flitted into his mind, and damned if it hadn't stayed there long after he'd gone to his own bed.

Sebastian waited until the fence was repaired and they were packing up the ute again before he raised the farm management issue with Liam. He worked on keeping his words civil and his tone even as they headed back to the house for smoko. "So tell me about these lambs."

"Don't worry, I wasn't keeping you out of the loop. When

I said I'd spoken to Pop about it, it was before you came home. I called him to ask about the wheat harvest and he brought it up." Liam's tone was conciliatory. "And Seb, I'm still learning the ropes, too. It's been a hard slog, and a long way from what I was used to doing in England."

"Okay. That's all right then. I was pissed off that you hadn't discussed it with me, but I'm sorry if I sounded short."

Liam turned his head slightly. "We haven't had much of a chance to plan things since you've come home. I think we need to sit down and sort out some sort of structure."

"Structure?" Sebastian asked.

"Yeah, what part of the farm you want to take over. You know when the harvest starts, and when the lambing's over. What you enjoy the most. There's no point taking on work that you don't enjoy."

Sebastian tried to look interested as he thought about what part of the farm work—if any—he enjoyed the most.

"Then we've got the extra cattle to worry about," Liam continued. "Not to mention the day-to-day maintenance of the place, keeping the accounts, and looking after the equipment."

Sebastian narrowed his eyes as he glanced over at Liam, but his cousin's face was innocent. "If I didn't know better, I'd swear you were trying to turn me off the place."

"Why the hell would I want to do that? I need your help." The ute rattled as Liam changed down a gear as they approached the cattle grate in the house paddock. "If you're thinking of not staying, you'd better make up your mind quickly."

It might have been his imagination, but there was something in Liam's tone. "Do you want me to go or stay?"

The surprise on Liam's face was genuine. Sebastian knew his cousin well enough to see that.

"I thought you might prefer to look after the place

yourself," Sebastian added.

"Don't be stupid. You're family and it's your right as much as mine." Liam parked the ute in front of the hayshed. "You've got as much right to make decisions as I have, and as Lucy and Jemima do. But you have to *want* to be here."

"So, let's throw that cat amongst the pigeons. Let's say one of us didn't want to be involved."

This time Liam's gaze was narrow. "What are you trying to tell me? You're thinking about going already?"

"Already?" Sebastian's temper fired. "Is that what you're expecting me to do, eventually?"

"No. I didn't say that."

"It sounded like it."

Liam strode off ahead of him to the house, where Gran and Pop were sitting on the front verandah.

"Kettle's boiled," Gran said as she stood slowly, looking from Liam to Sebastian. Her brow wrinkled in a frown.

Sebastian waited until she was inside before he followed Liam. "Let's not argue in front of Gran. She picked up on us straight away, the old witch. And before you say anything, I say that with love and respect."

"I wasn't aware we were arguing." Liam's expression was closed and Sebastian took a breath.

"I'm sorry for snapping at you. Let's sit down at your place tonight and make a plan."

"Okay, come over for dinner." Liam's face broke into a smile and Sebastian relaxed. "Unless you already have dinner plans?"

It had been too late to return Isabella's missed calls last night, and too early when he'd headed out to the paddocks at first light with Liam. Sebastian took the mug of tea that Gran had poured for him, and he pointed to his phone. "I've just got a call to make." He picked up a scone with jam and cream and ate it in one bite.

"Sebastian Richards! Manners!" Gran said and Liam smirked.

"Sorry, Gran. I'm in a hurry," he said around the mouthful of scone.

As he walked away, Liam called out to him. "Make sure you've swallowed that before Isabella answers the phone; otherwise, she won't understand a word you say."

Sebastian was tempted to make a rude sign in response to Liam's teasing, but he was aware of Gran's eagle eyes. Instead, he grinned. It was just like when they'd been kids and he and Liam had sparred, and Gran had chided them about their table manners.

He wandered over to the hayshed, wondering how Liam had known it was Isabella he was calling.

Am I that obvious?

With a shrug, he swallowed the last of the scone, pressed speed dial for her number, and smiled when it picked up immediately.

"Bella, it's Seb. Sorry I missed your call last night. What's up?"

"That's okay. Nothing's wrong. I was just ringing to see if Lucy dropped off all the wedding stuff okay."

"She did and it's safely tucked away in Gran's spare room. She said you had a good day in Dubbo."

"We did, although I spent way too much money and bought too many clothes. Your cousin is very persuasive."

"That's Lucy." Sebastian looked down as one of Daisy's pups crawled over his foot, and he bent down to pick it up before he put it back in the hay with Daisy. "What are you planning to do today?"

Her sigh sounded loud over the phone, and then she turned it into a cough. "Probably just help Dad in the milk bar over lunch."

"Over the Spring Downs lunch rush, hey?" he said. "How

would you like to come for a ride on my bike tonight? Get out of town for a while?"

She was quiet for a moment, and he held his breath hoping she'd agree.

"Yes, I'd love that. More location scouting?"

Damn. I am an idiot. He'd totally forgotten about going to Liam's. "No. I'm heading across to Liam and Angie's house so I'll come into town and pick you up." He was sure it would be okay with Liam. "I was going to call you, anyway, to see if you were free this weekend to go out bush and give me a hand with the cameras. It'll be my last chance for a while with the races the weekend after, and then the wedding."

Sebastian frowned. Actually, he was going to be busy with all this on his plate.

"I could drive out," she said.

"No. I'll come and get you. The bike needs a good run to clear the cobwebs."

After arranging to pick Isabella up at six, he sauntered back to the verandah and tucked his phone back into the pocket of his work shirt. Liam finished his cup of tea and headed for the ute. "Come on, we'll go and sort out these sheep."

As they drove out of the house paddock, Sebastian leaned forward. "Okay if I bring Isabella over tonight?"

To his credit, Liam didn't react apart from a simple, "Yeah, that'd be fine."

• • •

The time they spent at Liam and Angie's had been fun, although Sebastian had disappeared into the office with Liam for a good hour while Angie had shown her around the house and the newly planted garden. Isabella wasn't sure if she'd imagined it, but they'd both seemed a bit tense when they emerged, but the mood quickly dissipated—if it had even been there.

The ride home had been quick, and she enjoyed the feel of the cool wind rushing through her hair as the bike had eaten up the miles too quickly. Sebastian had seemed preoccupied, but he'd snapped out of it when they arrived at the apartment. Dad was still at the club playing in his weekly darts tournament.

"Would you like another coffee?" she asked as Sebastian stood there with his hands in his pockets.

"Yeah, sure, thanks."

The silence was easy between them as Isabella pottered around brewing the coffee and taking out some biscuits she'd baked earlier. It had helped pass the time, and Dad had taken most of them down to the milk bar when he'd smelled them fresh out of the oven.

"So are you looking forward to the races this weekend?" Sebastian broke the silence as she handed him the coffee mug.

"I am. I can't believe it's such a big event in such a small town."

"But it's a big area. You'll be surprised at how far and wide people come from to go to the races." He flicked her a teasing grin, and the butterflies in her tummy jumped. "Look at you, all the way from Italy."

She pulled a face at him. "The same could be said about you."

He shook his head. "Nah. I'm a local now."

Isabella looked at him curiously. "Do you mind if I say something? Maybe a bit personal?"

He lifted his cup and looked at her over the rim. "Go ahead."

"Don't take this wrong way. I feel like we've become good mates ever since you rescued me at the airport and I'd like to be honest."

He raised his eyebrows, and she regretted bringing up what she was thinking. "Yes, we have."

"It's just that you don't seem to be really happy out here. I saw the look on your face after you came out of Liam's study tonight, and you looked like you didn't want to be there."

Sebastian's eyes were bleak as he held hers. "You're more perceptive than any of my family, Bella. Except maybe for Gran, but hers isn't perception. It's just me fulfilling her expectations."

"What do you mean?"

"Gran doesn't think I've got the strength of character to stay here. Or the work ethic."

"That's not fair," Isabella protested hotly.

"It mightn't seem fair, but that's the way it is. And that's why I'm going to stay out here and prove myself. Not just to them, but to me, too." His words were quiet as he stared over the top of her head. "Maybe coming home was the worst mistake I've ever made, but I've got to suck it up and get on with it."

Isabella reached out to him. "But why do you have to follow what's expected? And is it really expected? Are you sure it's not something that you're putting too much importance on? Proving yourself on the farm? Is it that important to your family?"

He shrugged and her heart went out to him. He looked like a little lost boy, and all she wanted to do was hold him and make him better.

She squeezed his hand and then the old Sebastian was back with a wide smile. "How did we get so serious? Don't worry about me. It'll all work out. Changing homes and jobs is always stressful, and when I was a kid I loved being out at the farm. Forget what I just said. I'm fine."

"If you ever need a shoulder, I'm here."

"But not for much longer. You're going to be jetting off to follow your dreams." His voice was serious again. "And I'll be here rediscovering mine."

"Next time I come to visit, you'll be an old cowboy sitting on your horse with a tribe of kids behind you."

Why does that thought make me feel unsettled?

"Thanks for the coffee and the ear." He stood and pushed in his chair. "At least you've made me a very happy man, anyway."

"Oh? How's that?"

"You said you're going to come back and visit. Don't leave it too long, will you?" He ruffled his fingers through her curls. "I didn't go much on the 'old' cowboy tag, though."

For a moment, his finger lingered on her hair, and she caught her breath as she stared at Sebastian's mouth. No matter how hard she'd tried, she couldn't get the feel of his lips out of her thoughts, even though it had been a couple of weeks since he'd kissed her at the airport.

The moment passed when he turned and picked up his jacket from the back of the chair. "Do you want me to pick you up for the races on Saturday?"

"Like a date?" She smiled.

"Yeah. Like a date." His dark eyes held hers as he slipped the jacket on and chuckled. "Roses and the works."

For a moment she was very tempted and then shook her head as common sense kicked in. "Thanks, but no. With the dress and shoes I'm wearing, I'll need to go in Dad's car."

"This outfit has me interested." His voice held a sexy note, and he tried to waggle his eyebrows. "Tell me more."

Isabella giggled. "No, I don't want to see any more wiggling eyebrows. It doesn't suit you."

"Oh no." He placed a hand on his chest. "Now you've hurt my feelings."

"Time for you to go home, then. And you'll have to wait

till Saturday to see my shoes." She shook her head. "I still can't believe Lucy talked me into them. I'll see you at the races."

"Okay. I know when it's time to go. But seriously, Bella, I am looking forward to seeing you again."

Before she could reply, he dropped a kiss on her cheek. As he opened the door, she could hear Dad making his way up to the apartment.

"Maybe if I bring roses I can bring you home?"

"Who knows? You'll have to wait and see."

"Bring a spare pair of shoes, just in case."

"I'll see." He leaned over and brushed his lips on her cheek again as her father reached the top of the stairs, but even the crafty look on her father's face couldn't burst her little bubble of happiness.

She put her hand to her cheek as she followed Dad inside.

"You're spending a lot of time with Sebastian," he said.

Isabella straightened her back and went to the sink to rinse the cups.

"I am, aren't I?"

She could almost hear his hands rubbing together. If it made him happy, who was she to argue?

Chapter Sixteen

Saturday dawned bright and sunny but with a stiff cool wind from the south. Sebastian stood on the verandah, waiting for his grandparents to appear all ready to head to the Come-by-Chance seventieth anniversary race day. Gran had been in the kitchen, packing food for the picnic and in her usual fashion had hurried up the hall to get glammed up with only a few minutes to spare. Lucy and Jemima had volunteered to be the designated drivers, and Lucy and Garth were due to pick them up any minute.

"Hurry up, Gran. I can see the dust kicking up from Garth and Lucy's place," he called from outside her bedroom window. "They're on the way."

"I won't be long."

Pop wandered out to the verandah and Sebastian grinned. "Welcome to my life. The coach had to wait for your grandmother most mornings on our tour." His grandfather was dressed in a pale-grey suit with a black bow tie.

"You're looking pretty swish, Pop."

"I can't say the same about you, Seb." Pop looked him

up and down, and Sebastian looked down at his moleskin trousers and plain blue shirt.

"Hey, this *is* really dressed up for me." He'd put away the usual jeans and T-shirt and pulled out what he considered his good gear.

My country clothes. He wouldn't be seen dead in moleskins and cowboy boots in the city but it was funny; he felt comfortable in them out here in the Outback.

"You'll have some competition today, if you want to catch your lady's attention." Pop looked at him sideways. "There'll be stockmen and rouseabouts and property owners from Narrabri to Dubbo at the races today. It's going to be a ripper of a day."

"My lady?" He looked back at Pop curiously. "And what lady would that be?"

"Bella." Pop lowered his voice. "I shouldn't tell you this, but your Gran reckons Con's daughter's got her eye on you. If you play your cards right, you could be settled here like the others before you know it."

"I'm pleased to hear Gran has my future all sewn up." Sebastian folded his arms and leaned on the veranda post, waiting for Lucy and Garth to arrive. He shook his head.

Bloody Gran. She was an old meddler. He'd have to warn Bella.

"Don't get that tone in your voice. She only wants the best for you. She wants you to stay here and be happy." Pop looked at him anxiously. "Do you think you'll stay?"

"I'm here. And don't worry, I'll do the right thing." Sebastian smiled. "But Pop, it's good to have you home, too." He avoided answering the direct question. How could he say what his plans were when he didn't know what each day would bring? "How long till you pair head off on your next trip?"

Pop sighed. "I'd like to stay home for a while, but your

grandmother reckons it will cramp your style with a couple of oldies in the house with you. So we're off again next month."

"Where to this time? Somewhere exotic?"

Pop shook his head. "Exotic enough, but no more overseas. I put my foot down. If I have to travel, I want to see some more of our country. So we're going to the Northern Territory on a coach trip. I'm sick of being in planes."

Sebastian nodded. A plume of dust whipped into the sky from the direction of the back gate.

"Jeez, that wind'll blow a dog off a chain if it gets much stronger. It's not going to be very pleasant at the racetrack." Pop picked up his hat and pushed it onto his head.

"Harry Peterkin, by the time you settle at the bar with your old cronies, you won't even notice the wind or the dust." Gran pushed open the screen door and pulled the front door shut behind her.

"Woo hoo, Gran, look at you. All tarted up." Sebastian whistled.

"Manners please, Sebastian." But Gran smiled, and the colour in her cheeks deepened as she adjusted her hat.

"Help your grandfather with the eskies, please. I put them outside the laundry door," Gran said as Lucy pulled up in the driveway.

"Here, Pop. Pass it to me and I'll lift it in." Garth came around the back of the vehicle and hoisted the smaller esky into the back of the SUV, and Sebastian slid the larger one into the space beside it.

"You sit up front with Garth, Seb, and I'll ride in the back with Gran and Pop." Lucy got out of the car as Sebastian opened the back door for Gran. He held out his hand and helped her up into the high vehicle.

Sebastian peered inside the car. The baby booster seat wasn't there, nor was James. "Where's James?"

"Melinda, Jerry Ferguson's granddaughter, offered to

babysit for the day. She's a preschool teacher in town, and she didn't want to go to the races." Lucy smiled. "So I can have fun with the girls."

"Melinda will be the only one in the whole district not there today. But it's good that you can enjoy yourself without worrying about James, love," Gran said.

Sebastian climbed into the passenger seat in the front and looked back at Gran as Garth started the engine. "That esky was pretty light. That's not as much food as you usually take, is it, Gran?"

His grandmother waved a dismissive glove-clad hand. "Don't you worry about the food. It's all sorted. Come-by-Chance won't know what's hit it this year."

"Is it the same picnic as it used to be? It must be ten years since I came to one of these race meetings."

"Yes, everyone takes a picnic lunch, and we put it all out on the communal tables that will be set up. Still not allowed to take alcohol in; it's all provided at the bar."

"Okay." He looked suspiciously at Gran as she nudged Lucy. "So what's so special about the food this year? Did you learn some fancy *nouvelle cuisine* dishes while you've been in Europe?"

"Don't you worry. You won't starve. I've just brought a couple of lemon meringue pies for dessert. Bella's doing the rest."

"Bella?" He stared at his grandmother.

"Yes, Prickle Creek Farm is doing a gourmet lunch this year. I've been talking to Bella on the phone. I bought the ingredients, and she's prepared all of the savoury cold food."

Bella! Not Isabella. And Gran had been on the phone with her, arranging things. Very chummy by the sound of things. Gran was up to something. He was right to be worried after what Pop had said.

Sebastian turned his head to Lucy. She looked away, but

not before he caught her smile. Yes, the pair of them were definitely up to something. He'd put money on it.

"Look, there's Liam and Angie's car. They're waiting for us at the turnoff." Gran's expression was innocent as Sebastian turned back around to talk to Garth.

Half an hour later, the two vehicles were parked in a paddock next to the racetrack beside hundreds of other vehicles: cars, utes, SUVs, and work trucks as well as the occasional horse float standing high in the rows of cars.

As Lucy held out one hand for the car keys to put in her bag, she looked up and smiled at Sebastian. He wouldn't be surprised if they were having another baby. After all, according to Lucy, she was going to have six.

"So how come you volunteered to drive, Luce?" he asked. "I thought you were going to have a day with the girls. I know how much you love a champagne or two."

Gran smiled, Lucy nodded, and Garth's grin was wide.

"So do you have something to tell us?" he teased.

"Yep, a winter baby next year. So I'll be drinking soda water today." Lucy patted her flat tummy beneath the figure-hugging green lacy dress she was wearing. "And I won't be able to wear this dress for much longer."

"Not that there's much call for evening wear in Spring Downs," Sebastian said as he hugged Lucy and then shook Garth's hand. "Congratulations, mate."

But as happy as he was for Lucy and Garth, he repressed a shiver. Not the sort of life that appealed to him. He was a long way from being ready for fatherhood.

As they walked across the paddock to the gate leading to the track, Sebastian kept his eyes peeled for a canary-yellow Citroën.

• • •

Isabella stood in the large marquee next to the race club building that had been set up for the food. A series of *bain maries* lined the back wall, and power cords snaked up the tent posts and under the flap over to the small building. The smell of the warming food filled the air with enticing aromas. The items she'd prepared could stay in the coolers until lunchtime. She'd decided to forgo cooking hot dishes when Dad had told her that forty degrees had been forecast for the day. She was happy not to be spending the summer here. A memory of her school uniform sticking uncomfortably to her back in high school flitted into her mind. It was hard to summon up many good memories of living out here. But to be fair, the summers in Florence could get pretty hot, too.

Preparing the food for today had been a great practice run for next weekend's wedding. Isabella had been able to source all of the ingredients without much trouble—even the gourmet items—and Dad's small kitchen had been more than ample to prepare the hors d'oeuvres last night. It had been after midnight when she'd finished cooking late and added four large savoury flans to the cooler. She'd gone to bed satisfied that next weekend's catering would be just as easy. The wedding menu was finalised, and she had ordered the last items online last night while the flans were in the oven.

The quantities for the wedding were large like she was used to. Isabella had catered for events in her last job, and she would have plenty of helpers, according to Helena. She was really looking forward to doing what she loved. The kitchen at Prickle Creek Farm was a chef's dream. Better than some of the restaurant kitchens she'd worked in over the past few years. But even in the cramped space in Dad's small apartment, it had been good to get back to some real cooking.

"Isabella!"

She turned as her name was called over the noise of the crowd in the marquee. Dozens of men and women were unpacking eskies and coolers and portable refrigerators. The array of food beginning to fill the tables promised a sumptuous feast for the day ahead.

Lucy was walking towards her, a wide smile on her face.

"Lucy." Isabella stood and smiled back. "Wow, look at you. That dress looks gorgeous! And the hat is perfect!"

Lucy twirled in her high heels and then nodded at Isabella. "But look at you. Absolutely drop-dead gorgeous."

Isabella smoothed her fingers over the midnight blue fabric. "It is a beautiful dress. I love the feel of the silk against my skin."

Lucy nodded. "And the shoes are divine, and I'm so pleased you decided not to wear a hat. Your hair looks great like that. Did you book into Marcy's to get your hair done this morning?"

Isabella reached up and touched the pale-blue fascinator with the small net that she'd pinned to the top of her curls. "No. I did it myself. I had to send Dad to the supermarket for a can of hair spray to keep my hair up. This wind is so strong."

Lucy linked her arm through Isabella's. "Are you all sorted here?"

"Yes. I've got the table space reserved and the coolers are underneath. I just have to put the food out when it's time to eat."

"Great. Did your Dad drive across or did you?"

"Dad booked us on the bus from town." She couldn't help the soft smile. "He's so determined for me to have a wonderful day here. I think he really believes if I enjoy myself I'll consider staying."

Lucy shot her a curious look. "Would it be so bad?"

"Oh, Lucy don't you start on me. It's not going to happen. I'm only here for a few more weeks. As much as I love spending time with you all, remember I'm only visiting."

"I know. But I can still miss you when you go," Lucy

said as they walked out of the marquee together and Isabella looked around. "Come on, we'll get a drink. Garth and Liam were setting up the chairs for us fairly close to the bar."

Lucy pointed to a group of chairs, a few metres from the side of a small building that was covered with tree branches. Garth and Liam were arranging the chairs around a small table, but there was no sign of Sebastian.

But she wasn't going to ask.

"I wondered what that building was. It's the bar?" She and Dad had walked around the back of the small building to get to the food marquee a little while ago. "What's with the branches?" She put her hand to her hair and turned her head as a strong gust of wind blew dust into her face.

"Yes, it's the bar. The branches are there to make shade over the uncovered part of the verandah. Although in this wind I don't know how long they'll last," Lucy said.

A warm hand touched Isabella's elbow, and she waited for the wind to ease before she looked up into a smiling face.

"Hey there." Sebastian's smile was wide and she grinned back.

"Hello," she said. "Look at you. Out of your usual black gear. But you've still got the camera." She tapped the strap holding the camera firmly against that broad chest.

"I'll go and order our drinks while you keep Seb company." Lucy's smile was guileless. "Why don't you take Isabella's photo before the wind destroys her hair?"

Before either of them could answer, Lucy hurried across to the bar.

"That sounds like a good idea." His deep voice sent warmth blossoming in her cheeks, and then when he took her hand to lead her to the fence, her nerve endings skittered and her legs trembled.

"I love the sexy net over your face," he said. "Put one arm along the rail and half turn to me. Lower your head a bit and then look up through the net."

Isabella's face warmed even more as Sebastian's gaze roamed from the fascinator in her hair down to the ridiculously high-heeled shoes she was wearing. That was why her legs were shaking, it had nothing to do with the way he was looking at her.

"You don't really need to take my photo, do you?"

"Yes I do. I'm taking photos of every part of the races today. And you look beautiful, Bella. Love the shoes!"

"Thank you. It was fun getting dressed up."

His gaze skimmed over her as he lifted the camera. "Nice to see legs, too." His grin was cheeky and her tummy fluttered.

"Nice to see you out of a T-shirt for a change," she shot back. Although the looser shirt didn't do justice to the broad chest that she knew was underneath the crisply ironed cotton shirt. "And you look like a country boy."

"Don't wish that on me," he said, but his smile was wide. "Where's your dad?"

"Um." Isabella cleared her throat, her nerves tingling. "He found his mates from the club, and they went over to put a bet on."

Sebastian snapped off a couple of shots and then looked down at the camera. "Perfect!"

"Email me one. It'll be a good memory of this day when I'm back at work." Isabella looked around at the crowds of people streaming in the gate. She hadn't realised so many people lived out here.

"It will. You can reminisce about the Come-by-Chance races when you're over at Ascot hoity-toiting with the British."

"I'll be more likely slaving over a grill cooking for them." She looked at him as he took her arm again. "How did you know that The Three Ducks isn't far from Ascot?"

"I didn't. I was just teasing you." He gripped her hand

tightly as she almost stumbled. "I'm worried about you going over on this uneven ground in those heels. Do you want me to piggyback you?"

"Piggyback! That would totally take away from this elegance I spent all my money on. Just let me hang onto you till I reach a chair. These shoes were not such a good idea." She looked down ruefully as she negotiated the uneven dusty ground. "I was imagining a racecourse with paths and grass around it."

"You won't find that in the Pilliga Scrub, Bella."

"No. I guess it was a silly expectation."

He took her other hand. "Let me help you."

"Okay. I'm in your hands." She lowered her gaze and looked at Sebastian through the net. It was a long time since she'd flirted. She was having a lot of fun. He held her gaze, and she was glad of the support of his hands when an exquisite little quiver ran down her legs.

"Have you picked a winner for the day?" He nodded towards the stables as he led her through the crowd. The ground was even now, but he still held on to her hands.

"I haven't had time to think about it. I was getting the food out of the bus. We haven't been here long."

"Bus? That's why I didn't see your dad's car parked over there."

"Yeah, we came on the bus from town. Dad wants us both to have a good day."

"Well, we'll make sure you do." His voice lowered. "Listen, I hope Gran hasn't been bothering you."

"Bothering me? No, I was happy to help out."

"That's good, then. She can be an old witch when she wants her own way."

"Her own way?" Isabella frowned. "What does she want?"

Before he could answer, Lucy caught up to them, juggling

a can of beer, a can of soda water, and a glass of champagne. "I got one for you too, Seb."

"Thanks. Come on. We'll go and get settled." He held her hands firmly. "Hang on tight. This is where the ground gets rocky. Are you sure you don't want me to carry you?"

"I'm sure."

By the time they reached the group settled onto the chairs in front of the racetrack, Isabella was giggling. Sebastian had walked backwards as he guided her over the uneven ground. Every so often, he'd stop to chat and introduce her to someone he knew, or if he wanted to snap a photo, he'd make sure she was stable on her shoes, let her go, take the photo, and then take both her hands again.

By the time they'd negotiated their way over to the chairs and garnered a lot of smiles from the crowd on the way, it seemed natural when Sebastian slung his arm around her shoulder as they joined his family.

It felt warm…and nice.

Chapter Seventeen

"No way!" Helena's voice rose, and she tapped her fan on Liam's shoulder. "That old nag has no chance. Take my advice and put your money on Ted's 'Lucky Streak.'"

"Listen to your grandmother, Liam," Pop said. "That horse is going to romp it in."

Liam laughed and nudged Sebastian. "What do you reckon, Seb? I reckon old Sam would have a better chance than that old fellow of Ted's winning."

"I'm with Liam, Gran." Sebastian's eyes were twinkling. "You're gonna do your dough."

Helena folded her arms and smiled. "I've never once lost money at the races."

"There's always a first time." Sebastian laughed when he received a tap of the fan for that comment. "You've got no chance this year."

Happy banter and the opinions on the chances of each horse winning the J O'Brien Memorial Come-By-Chance cup filled the air as the family argued about which horses to bet on. As Isabella stood and listened to the men tease their grandmother, she felt a tap on her shoulder and Lucy squealed.

"Oh yes, Isabella." Her squeal was echoed by the congratulations of those around her as the man who had tapped Isabella made his way to a young woman sitting in the next group.

"What did that mean?" Isabella looked back at Sebastian who was standing behind her chair. Every time he leaned over to speak to Liam or Garth, his arm brushed her shoulder or his head was almost cheek to cheek with hers. A woodsy aftershave tickled her nose when he was close. "Lucy? Seb?"

"Sorry, Bella. What did you say?" Sebastian's breath whispered across her cheek as Lucy continued to jump up and down, clapping her hands.

"I asked what it meant when that man over there carrying the clipboard tapped my shoulder and Lucy squealed."

"I don't know." He turned to Garth. "Garth, what's Lucy so excited about?"

Lucy grabbed her husband's arm. "Gosh, I forgot none of you have been here before…or in Seb's case, too long ago to remember how it works." She held her hand up to high-five Isabella. "You've made the final of Miss Come-by-Chance. I knew you would!"

Before Isabella could protest, her father hurried across, grabbed her hands, and pulled her up. He flung his arms around her. Isabella tottered on her heels and Sebastian grabbed for her hand.

"Oh, Bella. Well done," her father said as he hugged her. "I'm so proud of you. In the final, you are!"

She was surrounded by the family group, either patting her on the shoulder or kissing her cheek.

"We haven't had a finalist since Lucy was in high school," Gran said. Soft fingers took Isabella's and cool lips brushed across her cheek; she was surrounded by Lily of the Valley perfume. She'd been about to protest that she didn't want to go in it until Dad had come over and hugged her. Now she didn't have the heart to disappoint everyone.

"Well," she paused and took a deep breath. "Thank you, everyone, you'll have to tell me what to do."

"Just stand there and look beautiful." Despite the hot wind, Sebastian's voice sent a shiver to her toes.

As she looked away, she noticed Gran and Lucy sharing a look.

• • •

The first two races had been run, and the judging was about to take place. The crowd was happy and his whole family, including Gran and Pop, had come over to cheer for Isabella as the judging took place. Sebastian lifted his camera and snapped the finalists standing on the small verandah of the tiny building that was the Come-by-Chance race club. In his opinion, Isabella was a shoo-in. But he was biased. The other women up there were elegantly dressed, too. But no one was as pretty as Isabella. He grinned, letting his gaze linger on her legs and down to those gorgeous shoes that had made it necessary for him to hold her hand for a good fifteen minutes as they'd walked through the crowd. He'd been hard-pressed not to puff out his chest as quite a few envious glances had come his way, and it was pretty clear that Isabella was with him.

And he was really happy by that. And the flirting had been mutual.

He lifted his camera and zoomed in on her face. Her eyes were wide and alight with happiness, and her lips were parted. A pink flush tinged her cheeks, and that sexy veil covering half of her face sent a rush surging through him.

It was a damn shame she wasn't here to stay, because he

was falling for her.

Yep, falling for her. He finally admitted it to himself. For the first time in his life, a woman was in his thoughts day and night. Up until now, his love life had been occasional with a rapid turnaround. He'd had a few casual relationships. Ever since he'd lost his mother he'd been hesitant about trusting his heart to anyone. But really, he had never been seriously tempted.

Until now.

He was pretty sure his interest in Isabella was reciprocated, and he lowered the camera thoughtfully. But she was leaving, so maybe he should pull back a bit with the flirting.

Why couldn't they have met when he was in Florence?

But then what was wrong with having a fling while she was here? That would get her out of his system and he could focus on the farm.

Maybe that's why he was having trouble settling down now.

Yes, that's it!

If he had a fling with Isabella, once she left, he'd be able to devote his attention to the farm.

He looked over at her, caught her eye, and gave her a thumbs-up as the judging spokesperson walked to the verandah and took the microphone.

The gorgeous smile she returned almost melted his heart.

No, not his heart. His heart was not involved.

• • •

Isabella stood self-consciously beside the other young women. She felt like a bit of a fraud, not being a local, but no one seemed to mind. The mood of the picnic races was happy, and a couple of girls she'd gone to high school with had come up and congratulated her as she'd made her way up to the platform. The MC blew into the microphone and it crackled and squawked. The crowd quieted as he held up his hand.

"I'm sure you're all keen to get to those picnic tables," he said. "But first we have to announce the winners for this year. They all look gorgeous, what do you think? How about a round of applause for these lovely ladies?"

Not only was there clapping but many a wolf whistle filled the air.

"First up, the winner of Fashion of the Fields is Jeanette Perkins. Well done, Jettie!"

Applause filled the air as the winning lady made her way to the front.

"Now, unfortunately, there can only be one winner of Miss Come-By-Chance, but we do have a lovely runner-up today. Erin Nickleby, you look stunning. Congratulations."

A surge of relief ran through Isabella, and she smiled as Shirley from the milk bar stepped up and presented the two women with a small posy of flowers.

Erin and Jeannette waved to the crowd as the cheers got louder.

Isabella held her fascinator as a huge gust of wind shook the building behind them.

"Now it gives me great pleasure to announce Miss Come-by Chance for 2017."

Sebastian was staring at Isabella, and she focused on him. He tipped his hat back and his dark eyes were intense as he held her gaze. The noise of the crowd faded as she stared back. He nodded slightly, and she shook her head. She really hoped it wasn't her.

"Isabella Romano. Congratulations!"

The smile on Sebastian's face got wider, and Isabella shook her head again. Oh my God, she was Miss Come-by-Chance. She lifted a trembling hand to her lips.

Shirley came over and put a ribbon over her shoulder. "Well done, love," she said in her husky smoker's voice. "Look at your dad. He's jumping up and down."

Isabella looked at her father and decided to enjoy the moment. It was an honour, and it obviously meant a lot to the locals. And it would be a story to tell.

After a flurry of congratulations, she walked across the stage clutching the huge bouquet of flowers Shirley had given her.

Lucy grabbed her in a tight hug. "See, I had great taste in helping you shop, didn't I?"

Isabella laughed and smiled as Helena and Harry stood on either side of her.

"Photo, please Sebastian," his grandmother called out. Once the photo was taken, she leaned in and brushed her lips across Isabella's cheek. "Well done, Bella."

Dad came in for a photo, too, looking so proud, Isabella couldn't help but smile.

Five minutes of having her photo taken with what seemed like dozens of people, the crowd thinned as they moved over to the picnic tables.

"Oh, I have to unpack the coolers," she said.

"We'll go and make a start. Come on, Gran," Lucy said.

"Sebastian, you help Bella over that rough ground again," Helena said and nudged Bella.

Sebastian walked over as the journalist from the local paper took her details. Isabella was conscious of his gaze on her as she answered the questions. Finally, it was done, and it was only Sebastian standing there with her. She watched curiously as he lifted his camera strap from his neck and put his camera carefully on the wooden floor.

"Is it flat already?" she said with a laugh. "Too many photos of me. I'm embarrassed."

He stepped closer and shook his head. "No, it's fine, but I

wanted to congratulate you properly."

"Properly?" She lifted her face as he put his arms around her.

"May I?"

Before she could reply, warm lips descended on hers, and he held her close against him. Isabella closed her eyes as Sebastian kissed her.

The rest of the world disappeared as he slid his lips slowly across hers. The noise of the crowd, the dusty wind, and the neighing of the horses in the stalls all faded as warmth suffused her.

After a full minute, she pulled her head back and he smiled down at her.

"Congratulations, Miss Come-by-Chance." His voice oozed sexy, and a lovely little quiver ran rampant in her tummy. Before she could reply, a shrill whistle came from the direction of the picnic tables.

"Go, Seb!" Liam's voice was full of encouragement. Isabella and Sebastian turned and she groaned. His whole family was watching.

And Dad.

Chapter Eighteen

The next week passed in a blur as the wedding preparations took up everyone's time. Sebastian had been kept busy on many errands for Gran, Angie, and Jemima, but he didn't mind. Every trip to town was another opportunity to call in and see Bella. Every night this week was taken up with rehearsals, dinners, and making sure his camera gear was right for the wedding, so there was no chance of taking her out anywhere. He'd called her a few times and knew she was as busy as everyone else with the wedding catering. Yesterday afternoon, he and Liam and Ned had driven into Dubbo to collect their monkey suits, as Sebastian referred to them.

"Do I really have to wear that?" he'd complained as they stood in the formal hire suit.

"Yep. You do."

"I've never worn a suit in my life," Sebastian said, staring at the light grey suit and white shirt.

But no arguments were accepted, and the three men headed back to the Prickle Creek Farm where Gran hung the suits in her wardrobe.

The next day when he was in for smoko, Gran asked Sebastian to go into town. "I need more strawberries."

Even though Bella was catering for the wedding, Gran had been cooking up a storm as well.

"I'll come, too. I have to go to the produce store," Liam said. Sebastian bit back a comment. If Liam was there, it would be a quick trip into town and straight back to work.

Liam dropped Sebastian at the IGA grocery store with a wide grin. "Say hello to Bella. I'm sure you'll be there as soon as you've got the strawberries for Gran."

"A milkshake wouldn't go astray," he replied with a smile.

"You'll be next, mate." Liam's grin was wide.

"Next what?" But he knew what Liam was getting at.

"In your own monkey suit."

"Not a chance."

. . .

Bella came down from the kitchen upstairs when Dad hollered up the stairs that she had a visitor. She wiped her hands on her apron and pushed her hair back into the cap she wore. She was back in full chef mode and loving it. Sebastian was waiting at the bottom of the stairs, and her heart kicked up a beat.

"Hi there," she said.

He leaned over and kissed her cheek. "Only a quick visit. Liam's picking me up in five minutes." He was carrying a bag from the grocery store.

"How's it all going out there?" she asked.

"It's a madhouse." Sebastian shook his head. "But everyone seems to be happy. Are you organised?"

"Yes." She tipped her head to the side. He looked hot and tired. "A milkshake?"

"Thought you'd never ask." His smile sent a quiver down

her back, and she tried to ignore it. All too soon, she'd be heading back overseas, and Sebastian was well aware of that. Besides, he'd kissed her on the cheek, not the lips.

Not that I'm disappointed. Not one little bit.

That explosive kiss at the races was the only time he'd kissed her properly, unless you counted the kiss at the airport. She knew he'd just been showing off when she'd won the title. The kiss had meant nothing more than "look at me, I'm kissing the winner."

She knew she was being unfair to him, but she wasn't being very honest with herself. It was too risky.

Isabella slipped behind the counter and made a milkshake for Sebastian while Dad chatted to a group of customers from a coach that had come into town late in the morning. She put the tall anodized milkshake cup in front of him on the table and pulled out the chair opposite.

"Thank you." She smiled at the look of utter bliss on his face as he sipped at the straw.

"Double ice cream?" he asked.

She nodded.

"You're a wonderful woman, Bella."

Again, that silly little quiver in her tummy. Maybe she needed to eat something.

He put the cup back on the table. "After all this wedding kerfuffle is done with, I can get back to taking the photos for my contract. Are you still okay to come out on the photo shoot with me the weekend after the wedding?"

"Sounds good," she said.

"I was talking to Liam about it before I came into town. He and Angie aren't going away for a couple of months, and he can spare me for an extra couple of days. That's if you don't mind having a long weekend away from your dad?"

"That's fine. I'm happy to help. Where are we going?"

"We'll be roughing it out on the other side of Narrabri, at

a place called Yarrie Lake. As well as a gorgeous landscape, there's an array of telescopes up there, and I thought I'd have a look at taking some photos there. There's a mountain, and there's a great view, if it's clear. Plus, it's not too far away."

"So we'll be camping?" she asked, tilting her head to the side.

"Yes. Have you got a swag?" Sebastian asked and then immediately shook his head. "Of course you won't have one. Don't worry. I'll borrow a spare one off Liam."

"Um, what's a swag?" she asked feeling a bit silly.

"I forgot you didn't live here for very long. You didn't ever go camping?"

"Uh-uh." She shook her head.

"A swag is a canvas bedroll with zips, a thin foam mattress. It zips up and it's waterproof."

"Luxury," she said with a smile.

"I'm really looking forward to getting out in the bush with my camera." He looked at his watch. "I'd better get back."

Isabella was really looking forward to spending time with Sebastian, too.

There was no harm in a holiday fling.

The scraping of the chair leg on the floor snapped her out of her thoughts.

"Liam will be chafing at the bit if I don't get out there." He picked up the bag of fruit, went to lean over towards her, and then must have changed his mind. Instead, he lifted his hand and nodded. "I guess I'll see you tomorrow bright and early."

"Dad and I are coming out this afternoon with some of the food." She followed him to the door and out onto the footpath. "Your gran actually asked me to stay the night."

Was that a flicker of interest in his eyes?

"And?"

She shook her head. "I said no. It's a family night."

He stood there staring down at her, and she was damned if she could figure out what he was thinking.

"Fair enough." He gestured to the ute coming along the street. "Here's Liam. I'll see you when you come out later."

"Okay. Bye."

Isabella stood staring after the ute as it disappeared around the corner. There was something different about Sebastian, but she couldn't put her finger on it. He did still want her to help with his photo shoot, though.

With a shrug, she headed back up to the kitchen.

Chapter Nineteen

As it turned out, Isabella didn't see Sebastian when she and her father called out to Prickle Creek Farm later that night. There'd been some problem over at Daniela, Ned's farm, and everyone except for Gran and Jemima was over there sorting out some issue. Ned and Jemima were heading straight to Sydney after the wedding, leaving the children with Ned's parents when they took a quick honeymoon to the north coast. So the farm had to be running like clockwork.

"My last chance to have a break for a long time." Jemima patted her stomach with a smile, and Isabella thought how beautiful she was. Even after travelling the world, and having a fabulous job, Jemmy was happy here in Spring Downs.

Dad had told her Jemima's story about ten times. Isabella was sure that it was another ruse to convince her to stay.

"Do you want to stay until everyone comes back?" Gran had looked at her shrewdly when Isabella asked where everyone was.

"No, but thanks anyway. We'll have to get going. I've still got some last things to organise before I come out tomorrow.

What time do you want me here?"

"As early as possible. Did you see I got the boys to move the portable cool room to the back of the laundry? It'll save you a lot of time tomorrow." Helena pointed to the small white building on wheels just visible through the kitchen window.

"That's great. Thank you." Isabella glanced around the huge country kitchen. "This is going to be a great space to prepare everything."

"The roster with the CWA ladies is on the fridge," Gran said.

"And Lucy and I have decorated the shed. Poor Angie's been at a conference all week." Jemima gestured to the door. "Do you want to come and have a look? The only thing we have to do—"

"The *CWA ladies* have to do," Gran butted in with a smile.

Jemima nodded. "...is to put the white tablecloths on about noon. The florist is coming with the flowers just after that."

"Is there anything else you need, Bella?"

She looked towards the laundry. "Just one tiny favour?"

"Yes?"

"Do you mind if I use your laundry to wash my chef uniform after we are finished? Dad's washing machine leaves more rust stains than it cleans the clothes."

"Of course. And you know we expect you to join in the celebrations, too."

Isabella shook her head. "No, this is your family time."

Helena smiled. "We'll see."

• • •

Just after seven the next morning, Isabella pulled up in the house yard of Prickle Creek Farm. Apart from the dogs barking at the bright yellow car, all was quiet. She unloaded the food from the car into the kitchen and then moved the Citroën so it was out of sight behind the hayshed. By the time there was any sign of life in the house, she had the ovens going and three pots bubbling away on the stove. She looked up as a movement in the doorway caught her attention. Her mouth dried, and she couldn't look away.

An expanse of glorious tanned bare chest filled her vision. Sebastian was standing there, bleary-eyed and running his hands through his hair. It was the first time Isabella had seen his hair loose and was surprised how much younger it made him look. As she looked more closely and took in the dark shadows beneath his eyes and the pale face, she smiled. It could have been the Simpsons satin boxer shorts that made him look youthful, too.

"Had a rough night, did you, Seb?"

He jumped and peered into the kitchen. "Bella? What are you going here?" His voice was raspy. "Is it morning already?" He winced as he stepped into the light.

"Um, I hear there's a wedding here today, and I'm cooking for one hundred guests."

He put his hand to his head again. "Sarcasm doesn't suit you."

"A hangover doesn't suit you," she shot back as she crossed to the stove and picked up the wooden spoon. She didn't hear him cross the room as she stirred the curried chicken. When she turned and came face-to-face with a bare chest, she lifted her eyes and tried to stay calm.

"Would you like a coffee?"

"I'd kill for one. Damn that Liam. He can put the drink away and come up roses the next morning. My head feels like it's got little men with jackhammers inside it."

"How about a headache tablet?" Isabella forced herself

not to run her hands over that smooth chest as she took his hand and led him to the table. "Sit down and I'll make you a strong black coffee."

"You're a lifesaver." She smiled and went about her preparations as Sebastian sat there and watched her. Self-consciousness flooded through her as he took in her chef uniform. If it had been anyone else, she wouldn't have noticed them, but every time she moved or bent over or stretched to the high cupboards, she was aware of him watching.

Finally, he stood and pushed the chair in and mumbled something about having a shower. As soon as he'd gone, Isabella relaxed again. As much as she could, while she tried to get the image of his broad bare chest out of her mind.

Isabella supervised the setting up of the flowers in the shed and then took over organising the CWA ladies when they arrived, getting them into teams to set tables and do the last-minute food jobs like whipping cream and putting the salads together.

Finally, it was three o'clock and Helena came into the kitchen, wearing a pale-blue suit with a posy of rosebuds on her lapel.

"All okay here? Everything smells delicious." She smiled as she looked around before she took Isabella's arm and steered her outside. "The girls want you to come and say hello before the ceremony. I said I'd come and get you."

Isabella followed her up the hallway, keeping half an eye out for Sebastian, but there was no sign of anyone until Helena opened the door to a huge bedroom. Lucy was pretty in pink, and Angie was wearing an oyster-coloured sheath that hugged her petite figure.

But it was Jemima who brought tears to Isabella's eyes. She shook her head wordlessly as she looked at the beautiful woman with the huge pregnant bump. Jemima wore the full bridal gown, with the veil and the train.

She smiled at Isabella. "The first time Ned and I got married it was in a courthouse with his kindergarten teacher. I wanted him to remember today as pretty special." She shrugged as Isabella kept staring and Gran wiped away a tear. "I guess I went a bit overboard," Jemima said.

"No, you didn't." Isabella hugged her. "You are stunning." She turned to the other three women. "You all look beautiful. I wish you all a wonderful day. And now I've got to get back to the kitchen." She rushed out before she started crying. She'd never been one to get emotional at weddings or envy the bride, but seeing the happiness in that room, and sensing the solidarity and friendship between the women, left her feeling empty. She hurried back to the kitchen and picked up a wooden spoon and took out her feelings on a jar of cream.

It got worse a few minutes later when Jenny, one of the CWA ladies, called them outside. "Quick, come and see. They're in the garden and the ceremony is about to start." As she spoke, the sounds of violin music drifted into the kitchen.

Isabella swallowed. She didn't want to see this, but conversely, she didn't want to not see it. Smoothing her hands over her uniform, and tucking her loose hair into her cap, she walked to the verandah and stood behind the group of women who'd been such a help so far today.

The family was in the garden. Guests sat on chairs that were positioned in a half circle on each side of the lawn where the celebrant stood with the men. An arch loaded with blooming roses and white tulle was positioned in the middle of the grass. Ned's children: Kelsey, Gwennie, and Ryan, stood beside him at the front, and Liam stood to the side. As Isabella's gaze reached the end of the group, her breath caught, and she'd swear her knees literally trembled.

My God.

Sebastian looked very different from the man who she'd given coffee to this morning. His dark hair was pulled back from his face. His pale-grey suit sat snugly on his broad shoulders, and he stood tall and proud, watching his family. He was absolutely gorgeous.

Isabella put her hand to the door as a jolt of feeling slammed through her. She was going to have to be very careful where Sebastian Richards was concerned.

Tears threatened as the music increased in volume and Jemima and Angie stepped out onto the lawn. Isabella was close enough to see the expression of love on both Liam's and Ned's faces. She brushed away the moisture from her eyes and shook her head impatiently as she turned back to the kitchen. She was here to do a job—not get all emotional.

Later that night she retreated into cowardice. It was safer than seeing him looking like that. Besides, she was filthy and hot. Once the meal was served and the kitchen was cleaned up, she stood for a moment listening to the happy voices and the music coming from the hayshed, before she slipped out to the car and drove quietly down the road. Luckily, some of the other guests were leaving so the car didn't get any attention.

She didn't even worry about washing her uniform. She just wanted to get home. Away from a good-looking man who made her feel something she wasn't used to, and away from the happy family whose happiness increased her loneliness.

Chapter Twenty

A week after the wedding, Isabella frowned as she pulled out two pairs of jeans, a couple of T-shirts, plus one for sleeping in, and a cardigan. If it was too cold, she could wear her leather jacket. There was no point being a fashion statement. It was a camping trip and she'd be working alongside Sebastian, carrying his gear, or whatever else a photographic assistant did.

A car pulled up outside, and she was surprised when she looked out of her window. Sebastian was climbing out of a high, white ute. She leaned forward and watched. He moved around to the back of the ute and adjusted the straps that held the load on the tray. In the back was a canvas roll, a blue esky, and a large crate that she assumed held all of his photographic gear. A warm feeling settled in her chest as the sunlight glinted on his dark hair when he looked up at her window. It was embarrassment at checking him out, that was why she felt so shaky. With one last check in the mirror, Isabella fluffed her hair with her fingers and grabbed her bag. She hadn't seen him this week; every time he'd called and invited her out, she'd come up with an excuse as she tried to forget the feelings that had overwhelmed her at the wedding.

She walked through the milk bar where her father was talking to Sebastian. His black jeans were snug, and she'd swear his biceps had gotten bigger since he'd been working on the farm. That damn shaky feeling ran down her legs again.

Dad winked as she came in carrying the carry-all she'd found in the cupboard.

"I hope it's okay to take this old bag, Dad. I found it in the linen cupboard. I didn't think my suitcase would be right for camping," she said, shooting a smile at Sebastian. "I thought we'd be on the bike."

He shook his head. "Now that I'm a farmer, I thought I'd better invest in a ute. Pop's old jalopy is a bit too unreliable, not to mention noisy. I don't think it would have got us that far."

"That's your ute?" She gestured to the road where the shiny ute was parked.

"Yep, brand-spanking new." He shook his head. "Feels funny. It's the first car I've ever owned."

"Did you trade your bike in?" she asked as Sebastian held his hand out for her bag.

"Hell, no. No way could I part with my baby."

Isabella's laugh bubbled up. She was so looking forward to this weekend. Even if it was work, it was going to be fun. And a completely new experience for her.

She leaned in to hug Dad. "You behave yourself this weekend. And you think about what we discussed. Promise."

He hugged her back. "I will, *cara*. I promise."

Sebastian put the radio on when they hit the main highway north and groaned when a country and western channel blared out. "See if you can find some decent music," he asked with a smile over at Isabella.

"What do you consider decent music?" She leaned forward to peer at the dashboard. The sun was low in the sky, and bright shards of silver light were glinting through the line of clouds low on the horizon. "Not country and western, I take it."

"You're right. I hate it." He rolled his eyes. "Would you believe Pop still plays his old vinyl records on a turntable every night? If I hear 'I Want to Have a Beer with Duncan' one more time, I might have to resort to a beer or two myself!"

Isabella found the scan button and snatches of different songs floated through the cabin. Every time a different song played, she turned to Sebastian, and every time he shook his head.

On the fifth shake of his head, she shook her own head with a grin. "Okay, tell me what sort of music I'm looking for."

"Mellow music."

"That really helps. What sort of mellow?" she asked. "Classical or seventies mellow?"

"Seventies would be good."

She kept scanning until he nodded.

"That's good. Thank you." He turned to her briefly. "So don't tell me you're a country and western fan?"

"No. I'm not. This is nice." She nodded and hummed along with the slow music playing.

"Oh, I meant to tell you," he said. "I couldn't get a swag from Liam."

Isabella sat up straight, suspicion forming in her mind. "So? What does that mean?"

"It's okay. I've got mine. You can have that, and I'll build a fire and sleep outside. I just didn't want you to see the double one on the back of the ute and jump to the wrong conclusion."

"What sort of conclusion?"

"Um. That I was trying to share my swag with you. Liam said he sold his before he went to the UK and hasn't bothered to get another one. I thought he'd have it in his shed, but he downsized when he moved away." Sebastian flicked the headlights on as low trees arched over a particularly narrow section of the road. "I tried Garth, but they were out."

"It's okay. I wouldn't have thought the worst of you," she said. "I think I know you well enough now to know you always do the right thing."

"I try to." His voice was soft. "But it's damn hard sometimes."

"What do you mean by that? You'd like to share the swag with me?" Isabella frowned, ignoring the little flutter in her tummy.

Sebastian laughed. "That goes without saying, Bella. But we still haven't had a real date. And if I remember correctly, you don't succumb to any proposition until the second date. Unless I'm allowed to count the roses you brought last week as a date."

Isabella couldn't hold back the peal of laugher that bubbled out of her lips. "Succumb to any proposition? Have you been reading your grandmother's Regency romances, Seb?"

She looked over at him and he rolled his eyes. "My God, I'm even starting to sound like Gran. Next you know I'll break out into a rendition of 'The Pub with No Beer,' like Pop sings in the shower every night. I have to find a place of my own," he muttered.

"So you are going to hang around here?" she asked.

"Looks like it." It was hard to read the tone of his voice, but he stared ahead and there was no more conversation as they headed north.

• • •

Sebastian stood next to the ute parked on the grass on the edge of Yarrie Lake. The office was run by caretakers and they'd closed for the night, but an envelope stuck to the door with his name on it had confirmed the booking and directed them to the site they'd been allocated. The camping ground was huge, and they drove a couple of kilometres around the lake until the headlights illuminated a white post with number 31 on it, the site number they'd been looking for. It was pitch dark and they'd passed no other campers as they'd skirted the lake. Across the other side, a couple of fires flickered in the dark, reassuring him that they were not the only campers out here.

"It's very isolated," Isabella commented as she pulled a thin cardigan around her shoulders.

"I'll get a fire going. Grab my leather coat. It's on the back seat," he offered. There was no moon and a strong, icy wind was blowing in from the west. It was blowing so hard, it had slammed the ute door shut as soon as he'd let it go. "And then I'll get the billy boiling. Gran packed some sandwiches that we can toast in the jaffle iron."

"A fire?" Her voice was sceptical. "In this wind? Maybe it would be easier to eat them cold and go to bed." Isabella yawned and Sebastian reached over and took her hand.

"Trust me, Bella. I was a Boy Scout. Look, there's a fire pit over there and a pile of timber. I'll have a roaring blaze going in no time. You grab a camp chair and sit on this side of the ute, out of the wind, while I unload."

"No, I'll give you a hand. It'll be quicker." She shivered and he rubbed her hands between his. "And it'll warm me up a bit."

"It's a lot colder than I thought it would be." He looked up at the sky, but it was too dark to see if the clouds were threatening rain. There were no stars and that wasn't a good sign. If it rained, he'd have to sleep in the front of the ute; it would be cramped but better than getting wet.

Together they unpacked the back of the ute, and Sebastian quickly unrolled the swag and secured it to the ground. There was a cover that he rolled out over it and pegged down as well.

"I can smell rain," Isabella said. Almost as she spoke, the sky opened and a solid wall of rain descended.

"Quick, get in the swag," Sebastian yelled over the noise of the fat raindrops bouncing off the ground. As she disappeared into the small tent, he grabbed the esky and pushed it inside before crawling in with her. If it had been dark outside, it was pitch dark in here. He felt around for the LED lamp that he'd unpacked and pulled his hand back quickly when it touched a soft curve.

"Oops, sorry. I was looking for the light."

Light flooded the cosy space when Isabella located the torch and switched it on. She was sitting cross-legged and her eyes were dancing in the soft light. She grinned widely.

"Great weather to take photos," she said.

"Great weather to camp out," he replied.

"Great weather to sleep outside," she came back with.

"I'll sleep in the ute." He tried to inject enthusiasm into his voice, but the prospect was not enticing for his six-foot-two frame.

"Don't be silly. You can sleep in here. There's plenty of room for both of us." Her voice held laughter. "But so long as you know it's not a date. Just a camp out."

"Damn, I knew I should have packed the roses." He nodded slowly. "It's almost a date, you know," he said hopefully. "That light's as soft as a candle and I've got a bottle of white wine on ice in the esky."

Isabella folded her arms and shook her head with a giggle. "No roses. No date."

Sebastian looked at her in the soft light and caught his breath. Her lips were full and rosy, and a slight flush tinged her cheeks. Her black hair tumbled down in a riot of curls as she stared back at him…for a long time. Her brown eyes were framed by thick lashes and her lips parted softly as he held her gaze.

"What's wrong?" she asked after a long silence.

He knew his voice was husky, and he was surprised she couldn't hear his heart pounding in the small space of the swag.

"I'm just cursing myself for forgetting the roses," he said softly. "You're a very beautiful woman, Isabella."

She leaned closer as he spoke and her perfume surrounded him.

Lemons. Citrus. Sharp.

Her lips were close to his, but she didn't touch him.

"Maybe since you brought the wine and the almost candle, we could say it was half a date?" Her lips were so close, her breath warmed his cheek. He waited, not wanting to make the first move and break the date deal, but before he could move back, soft lips brushed against his.

Gently, ever so gently.

He reached around and cupped the back of her neck in his hand, increasing the pressure of her lips on his by nudging her head forward a little. When she didn't move away he closed his eyes and lost himself in the glorious warm softness of her mouth.

Never again would he smell lemons without thinking of this beautiful woman in this cosy space.

As her lips opened and she wrapped her arms around his neck, the torrential rain eased and gradually faded away into silence. All Sebastian could hear now was her soft breathing.

He opened his eyes as Isabella pulled back and rested her cheek against his.

"Are we going to have dinner?" she asked. He could feel her lips tilting in a smile against his cheek. "I'm starving."

"I guess we'd better." He moved back and reached for the esky. "How do you fancy cold sandwiches?"

"I'm starving, so it sounds good."

"Gran's homemade bread makes them gourmet quality."

The normal conversation dispelled the intimacy that had surrounded them moments earlier. Sebastian had been wondering how far he should take the moment, what her expectations were, but he was following Isabella's lead.

"Do you want to eat in here or go back outside?" he asked.

"Everything's going to be pretty wet out there, isn't it?" she said.

"Yep, the chairs will be soaked. So it's here, or in the ute."

"This is cosy and dry." She looked around. "Do you think the rain's gone?"

"I'm hoping it was just a localised storm. It wasn't forecast when I looked at the weather site before we left." He passed her a packet of sandwiches. "Would you like a wine with your meal, madame?"

She nodded as she unwrapped the sandwich. "I would, thank you."

"Unfortunately, I didn't pack the crystal flutes. We've only got the plastic mugs in the picnic set."

"I think I can cope."

Sebastian propped up a couple of pillows and leaned back after he'd poured the wine. He lifted the plastic mug and held it against hers. "To our first date," he said with a smile.

She lay beside him and they chatted. He had his head at one end of the swag and she had hers at the other.

Later, as he organised their pillows, he said, "Makes it like a twin bed. That okay?"

"That's fine. It's ages since I camped out." Curling up

close to him was tempting but Isabella stayed firm. It was bad enough that she'd kissed him before.

"Where did you camp?"

"A few of us did a tour of the Cote d'Azure when we finished at cooking school in Rome," she said. "We were all broke, but we had the opportunity to visit some of the top restaurants there, so we had a couple of old vans and a tarpaulin and we had the best time." She stared into the dark. "That was the last holiday I had. Five years ago."

"Sounds like you work hard." The nylon of the sleeping bag cover rustled as Sebastian stretched out. "Tell me about your new job. It's sounds like you're on the successful chef path now."

She bit her lip. If she agreed it sounded as though she had tickets on herself, but that was not her motivation for wanting to get to the top. It was hard to say what motivated her without sounding as though she was critical of what she picked up as Sebastian's more casual approach to life.

"I guess," she said after a long silence, "it's not because I want to be at the top, it's more because of how I've planned my life out." She rolled over on to her stomach and propped her chin in her hand. "I guess I've never left things to chance. It was hard being pulled from pillar to post when I was a kid. Mum and Dad were always moving. You know, we'd lived in seven different countries before Dad bought the milk bar and we moved to Spring Downs."

"Wow. You've seen a bit of the world then. I didn't leave Spring Downs until I finished high school." But Sebastian's voice held sympathy rather than envy.

"I did. And it made me absolutely firm in setting some pretty clear objectives for what I wanted out of my life, and putting them into a plan. A certainty that my life would go where I wanted it to. Not where a whim, or a fancy, or the lure of change would take me. I suppose you think that's a bit rigid."

"No," he disagreed. "But I do believe you have to be open to change, if something comes up. Take me, for example. All I wanted to do was see the world. Roam around with my camera and go where the whim—or the contracts—took me. And look at me now. Change happened. Gran called us home and here I am. A cattle farmer, back where I started."

"Maybe that's not such a bad thing. I really don't think that a hit-and-miss approach to life is the best way to live. It still surprises me that Dad has stayed here so long." Isabella gestured to make her point and then realised he couldn't see her. She switched the light on and looked at him.

Bad move.

Sebastian's eyes were shadowed in the dim light of the swag. He was propped up on the pillows and his T-shirt was bunched up. A glimpse of tanned skin beckoned below his T-shirt and Isabella wished she hadn't turned the light on as a rush of need fluttered in her tummy.

How easy would it be to have a night together? But could she walk away with no regrets?

No, that is not *a part of my plan.*

"I guess the bottom line is that you'll have to hope that it all works out and that you're happy here," she said faking a yawn. "I guess if we're going to get some sleep, so we can work tomorrow, I need to stop with the deep and meaningful stuff."

"Probably should get some sleep." His voice was soft. "But thanks for the insight. I can see where you're coming from. And Isabella, I want you to know how much I admire you for knowing what you want out of life."

As she drifted off to sleep she wasn't sure if she heard properly, but she swore that after a few minutes he added softly, "I wish I did."

Chapter Twenty-One

The sound of birdsong woke Isabella early the next morning. She rolled over and opened her eyes. She was alone in the swag. Sitting up, she fluffed her fingers through her hair and rubbed her eyes. She'd slept surprisingly well. The foam mattress had been soft, and the swag was warm and dry. Once Sebastian had turned the light off after they'd finished the sandwiches that his grandmother had packed, and half a bottle of wine, they'd lain there and talked for what seemed like hours. When he'd held the bottle up and offered to pour her a third mug of wine, she'd shaken her head. It had been hard enough to think about sharing a bed with him, without the added relaxation of more wine. Isabella knew it wouldn't have taken much persuasion to do more than sleep beside Sebastian but kissing him last night had been a spur of the moment thing, and while she had no regrets, she still wasn't sure about taking their relationship that one step further. She only had another week and a half here, and she didn't want to complicate matters.

As she poked her head through the opening, she was

greeted by a cheerful voice. "Morning, lazybones."

She clambered out—not very gracefully— and looked around. She was not a morning person, but she could still enjoy the view. The sun was shining and the grass was dewy and glistening after the rain of last night.

Sebastian pointed to a brick building a few hundred metres away. "Take my ute if you want to. The amenities block is a fair walk."

"I'll walk. She reached into the swag and grabbed her toiletries bag and the towel she'd packed. "Which way's the lake?"

"Um. I think we've made a big mistake. Or I have." His voice was serious, and Isabella turned around with a frown as she tucked the towel under her arm.

"A mistake. The photos you mean?"

"No." He shook his head. "The photos will be perfect. That rain has washed the bush clean, and the colours will be amazing. I mean the lake." He gestured to the lush green grass in front of them. As Isabella's gaze followed the direction of his arm, a couple of kangaroos hopped across the middle of the grassed area. "See that sign?" he said, pointing to a sign at the edge of the huge expanse of grass.

She wandered over curiously and then laughed as she read the words: No DIVING OR JUMPING FROM THIS JETTY. SHALLOW WATER. She turned around as he chuckled.

"This is the lake?" she said. "Where's the water?"

"Yep." He nodded with a sheepish look. "I guess there hasn't been enough rain up this way."

"Could make an interesting photo for your contract, maybe."

"Nah, not a lot happening out there apart from the odd kangaroo or two." He shook his head ruefully. "Go and have a shower, and we'll head to town for coffee and then up the mountain."

Isabella smiled as she headed to the amenities block. Very different to Lake Como where she'd worked before she'd gone back to Florence. She wondered how long Sebastian would last out here in this strange and different Outback landscape.

• • •

Sebastian sat on the now dry camp chair, camera in hand as he watched Isabella walk back from the amenities building. He'd rolled the swag up and secured it with the other gear in the back of the ute. They'd camp somewhere different tonight.

The gentle wind lifted her curls as she walked along the grass, and a wrench of need twisted through him. Last night when he'd lain at the other end of the swag from her, after she'd kissed him, it had taken every ounce of his self-control to stay there. Then he'd woken at first light and felt guilty as he'd watched her sleep. For a few moments, he'd given in and let his gaze linger on Isabella's face. Her hair was a cloud of black curls around her head. One hand was tucked between her rosy cheek and the small padded mat, and her lips were parted in a half smile as she slept. It was as though he was stepping over a privacy boundary so he'd slipped out quietly and gone for a walk with his camera.

He was satisfied with some of the wildlife shots that he'd taken, but it wasn't the sort of thing that would fulfill this contract. His heart wasn't in it today. His heart, and a great bucket of need, were back in the swag with Isabella.

He'd known her for a little more than a month, and he was starting to realise how much he was going to miss her when she left. Maybe bringing her along on this trip had been a mistake.

Maybe he was getting too serious, too quick.

Then again, maybe they should get together, get it out

of their system. A spring fling, and then both could move on with their real lives.

Maybe he should enjoy the time they had together before she went away.

No commitment, no serious intent.

Just a good time with a beautiful woman.

He nodded to himself as he stood to meet her as she reached the campsite.

"All ready to go?"

"Where are we off to, oh fearless camp leader?" Her smile was wide, and it was all Sebastian could do not to take her into his arms and run his lips over that luscious mouth.

"We're going up a mountain." He lifted the chair and put it in the back of the ute. "First we're going to find breakfast, and then we're going up Mt Kapatar."

"Sounds like fun. Is there climbing involved?"

"No. The brochure said we can drive to the very top."

She laughed and a ripple of warmth lodged in his chest. He clenched his hands around the car keys. "The same brochure that said this was a lake?"

He laughed. "Apparently it is, some of the time."

"Okay, take me to this mountain."

Three hours later, after a hearty breakfast—just in case there is climbing involved, Isabella had said as they placed their order—and a drive through beautiful green paddocks past interesting rock formations, they pulled up at the carpark at the lookout on top of Mt. Kapatar.

"No climbing." Sebastian pointed to the sign. "The lookout is one hundred metres away, so you're going to have to get your exercise elsewhere."

Isabella shivered as she climbed out of the ute. "It's

freezing up here." She reached back inside, and Sebastian passed her jacket over before he climbed out.

"I'm going to get you working now, so you'll warm up quickly."

"Okay, tell me what I have to do."

He opened the back door and sorted through his equipment on the back seat until he was satisfied that he had selected the lens he needed. He lifted the tripod with the extendable legs, and his fingers brushed against Isabella's as he passed it over to her. "Can you carry this for me?"

She nodded and took it off him. "Sure can. Anything else?"

"No. I'll bring the rest. I'll need you to hold the lens and the caps once I start changing them up there. I think the light's going to be good."

She set off ahead of him to the wooden stairs that led from the carpark up to the lookout. By the time they both reached the top, she was laughing. "Did the brochure say the hundred metres was all steps?"

Sebastian caught his breath. Isabella had run up the stairs like a mountain goat and was barely puffing. "No. I'll put you in charge of picking the location the next trip we take."

"I'd love to. That'll give me something to do for the next couple of weeks." He turned as she drew a breath and sighed. "Oh my goodness. Just look at that view!"

Isabella put her arms out and spun in a circle. It was hard for him to take his eyes from her as she pointed to the landscape that surrounded them in a 360-degree arc. Her jacket was open, and her T-shirt moulded her soft curves. Her expression was full of life, her eyes wide, and her mouth tipped in a huge smile.

"It's absolutely stunning," she said.

Sebastian cleared his throat. "The brochure said you can see ten percent of New South Wales from this lookout."

She was absolutely stunning. He'd barely looked at the view. He lifted his camera and checked the light to take her out of his sight.

"Look at the colours." Isabella shivered as she came over to stand beside him; he couldn't help putting his arm around her shoulder.

"Warm enough?" he asked as she led him over to the edge of the cliff where a low fence divided the open area from a huge drop.

"I am now."

"Beautiful," he murmured softly. Far below were green plains dotted with the occasional farmhouse, stands of bush, and the never-ending rows of wheat fields. In the distance, a small town edged the plain, and it was so clear you could see the red roofs of the houses. Isabella's hair brushed his chin, and the lemon fragrance surrounded him. He closed his eyes, inhaling her scent as she pointed out different features.

"Is that Narrabri over there? Do you think we can see Spring Downs from here?"

He opened his eyes as she turned beneath his arm and intercepted a curious look.

"Are you okay?" Her brow wrinkled in a frown.

Sebastian brought his mind back to the job in hand. This wasn't the right time to broach his idea of a spring fling.

Maybe later.

"Yeah, I'm just planning the composition of the photos." He knew his voice was clipped, but he needed to focus on something other than Isabella. They were all alone and hadn't passed a single car on the way up.

"Okay, let's get to work then." She left him, picked up the tripod, and extended the legs.

You can do this. Get to work. Take your mind out of your pants.

Lemons. He'd never go near them again.

Chapter Twenty-Two

Once Sebastian started to work he was totally focused on what he was doing, but he still found the time to explain the use of the different lenses to Isabella as she passed them to him. She was learning a lot, but once the equipment was set up, he didn't need her so she sat at the table, watching him compose the shots.

She was watching Sebastian the man. He was tall, broad shouldered, and well-muscled. His fingers were long and precise as he held the equipment. In the sunlight, muted by the lacy leaves of the branches, he was shadowed. The angled planes of his face were softened by the filtered light. As he looked at the landscape, he occasionally lifted his arm and ran his hand through his hair. He'd shed his leather jacket when the sun grew warmer, and Isabella sighed as his muscles flexed as he moved.

Her mouth dried when he ran the tip of his tongue around his lips, totally unaware of her watching him. His lips were full and she'd enjoyed the feel of them against hers last night. It was all she could do now not to go over, grab his face with her hands, and taste his lips again.

Dio, what is wrong with me? Was she so bored here in the Outback that she was fantasising about a man who was her friend?

But she began to walk towards him. *Damn the consequences.*

She was saved from making a foolish move as laughter came from the carpark, and a family appeared at the top of the steps. Isabella drew a deep breath and focused on bringing her raging hormones under control as the two adults and three children smiled at her. She sat back down at the table and watched the family as they exclaimed over the view.

The clouds began to move in from the south as Sebastian worked, and by late afternoon, Isabella had her jacket pulled tightly around her and shivered every time the wind gusted. When the first raindrop hit the camera, Sebastian looked up with a frown.

"I didn't see that weather coming." He shoved his camera in the carry bag.

"It came over quickly," she agreed.

The wind was icy, but he didn't seem to notice how cold it was until he looked over at her. She was shivering and fighting to keep her teeth from chattering. "Oh, Bella. I'm sorry. You should have said something. You look like you're freezing."

She nodded. "I am."

He quickly packed up the rest of the gear and then picked up his coat and passed it to her. "Here, put this on."

She didn't argue as he put it around her shoulders and then slung the camera bags over his. By the time they reached the car, the wind was howling and the rain falling steadily.

She climbed into the ute as he stowed his camera gear on the back seat. "So much for the heat of the Outback," she said with a grin.

"Not much of a night for camping, either," he said,

starting the car.

"Maybe the weather will be better off the mountain," she said hopefully. She'd be disappointed if he suggested going home early.

"Fingers crossed." He flashed a smile, and she grinned back.

Sebastian took it slowly down the mountain. Visibility was low, and the wind was buffeting the ute. Isabella bit her lip as the wheels slid at one point and the vehicle went precariously close to the edge of the cliff. She glanced over at Sebastian; his hands gripped the steering wheel, and he was totally focused on the road ahead. But as they turned the last corner at the base of the mountain, they were bathed in brilliant sunshine.

"Looks like we'll be able to camp after all. That bad weather was only up high."

She shrugged, not wanting to show how pleased she was to hear that. "It won't matter if it rains anyway. We were snug and cosy last night."

"We were." His face lit up in a grin as he looked across at her. "What sort of camping do you fancy tonight, apart from being dry?"

"What do I fancy tonight?" She tapped a finger on her lips and looked at him from under her lashes. "What does the brochure suggest?"

"Forget the brochure. Let's go for a bit of local knowledge." He changed up a gear and the speed of the ute picked up as they hit the bitumen road. "We can camp close to the telescopes or there's a camping spot near the river to the east where we could have a fire."

"Let's go for the river. You might get some good night shots, and then we can go to the telescopes tomorrow. How does that sound?"

• • •

Sebastian was pleased that Isabella chose the river option. Even more so when he turned off the main road and the camping ground was deserted.

"Looks like the rain has scared off all, bar the most intrepid explorers."

"Intrepid explorers? Where are they?" She looked around with a put-on smile, before she turned back to him. "All I can see is a chef and a photographer."

"A chef and a cow farmer," he corrected her.

"That sounds like one of those reality TV shows."

He parked the ute close to the river and smiled as Isabella jumped out and ran over to the shingly stones at the edge of the water. "Oh, quick, get your camera. It's gorgeous."

He reached for his camera and walked across to where she was standing, her eyes wide and her lips parted. It was the light that hit him first as he followed the direction of her finger.

The sun was close to the horizon, but it wasn't until Isabella grabbed his hand and pulled him over to the water's edge that he could see what she meant. A weeping willow swooped gracefully to the water, and between the softly draping branches, an old timber railway bridge was silhouetted by the setting sun.

"Quick, or you'll miss it." Her voice was filled with the same excitement that hit him as he lifted the camera and clicked.

A second or two later, the sun slipped behind the hills, and the tree and the bridge held no more magic. Sebastian pushed his camera over his shoulder to rest against his back and reached out for Isabella. His arms went around her, and he dropped a light kiss on her lips. "That, my dear assistant, was absolute perfection."

She tipped her head back and looked at him as her arms slipped around his neck. Her eyes were intense and her expression serious. For a long moment, he stared at her and she didn't move. Her brown eyes held a question, and he lifted his hand and ran his thumb gently over her lip.

"Isabella?"

She slid her hands down his shoulders and gripped the tops of his arms. "Yes, Sebastian?"

"What do you want to do first?"

"Maybe we should put the swag up in case it rains?"

He looked up at the sky. There wasn't a cloud to be seen. "I think that's an excellent idea."

She held his hand as they walked over to the ute and he put his camera away. He pulled the swag off the back of the ute, and by the time he'd unrolled it, Isabella had the groundsheet spread on the soft grass next to the water. She looked up at him, and his breath caught in his throat as she smiled up at him

A wicked, sexy, inviting smile.

"Haven't you got that swag up yet?' Her voice was husky and he fumbled with the strap, tempted to disregard the swag and lie down beside her on the groundsheet. The air hummed with tension as she stood and waited while he undid the clips on the swag. As he leaned over to pull it up, a teasing finger ran down the back of his shirt. He turned; Isabella was close behind him, her breath warm on the back of his neck. It was either that or the fact that she'd now managed to pull his shirt from the waistband of his jeans and her fingers were playing over the bare skin of his lower back that sent a shiver skittering down his arms.

He groaned. "If you want protection from the weather, you'd better stand over there where I can't reach you so I can concentrate on getting this swag up."

"Get the swag up?" Her grin was cheeky, and he shook

his head at her double entendre.

"I don't think you're going to have any trouble, um, getting the swag up, are you?" Her voice was low and husky, and it was all he could do not to reach out and take her in his arms.

"Bella. Behave."

This time her eyes were innocent. "Why?"

Sebastian grinned back at her and tried to steady his hands as he pulled the tent pegs from the small bag. It only took ten minutes to get the swag up and secure the pegs, but it felt like an hour to Sebastian.

He stood back and gestured to the swag. "Madame, your room is ready."

Isabella smiled, and her tongue peeked through her rosy red lips as her eyes held his.

"May I kiss you first, kind sir, to say thank you for finding me such a lovely place to stay?"

Her eyes were dancing as he held his arms open. "You can."

Isabella's breasts were soft against his chest. He closed his eyes, and her soft groan matched his as he lowered his mouth to her lips.

"Are you sure?"

"I am." Her words vibrated against his lips, and for a moment, he forgot everything else as he lost himself exploring her mouth. She sighed as he moved down to kissing the soft skin of her neck, and his hands explored the soft curves under her T-shirt.

"I've just got to go to the car," he said. "You get in there in case it rains." He looked up at the cloudless blue sky. "Hurry up. You don't want to get wet." Heat raced up his neck as she raised her eyebrows.

"Don't I?" she said with a wicked grin.

The sexy giggle that followed him made him hurry all the

faster to the car to get the packet he'd put into his backpack.

Just in case.

Be prepared. He hadn't been a Boy Scout for nothing.

"Don't worry. I've got enough fire to last me for a few hours. I can keep you warm," he said.

He grinned as he thanked the stars that he'd had the foresight for "just in case" as he crawled into the swag behind her.

Isabella's eyes were bright in the dim light, and he stretched out beside her. After putting the small packet under the pillow, he propped himself on one elbow and smiled down at her.

"Now where were we?"

"Didn't you say you were hot?" Her giggle almost curled his toes. "Maybe you've got too many clothes on?"

"You look very warm, too. Maybe I could help you take your T-shirt off?"

She nodded and he slid his hand down to her waist. Her skin was warm beneath his fingers. Seb lowered his head and nuzzled her neck. "*Mmm.* Warm, very warm. Definitely need less clothes on." He was finding it hard to get the words out.

Isabella lifted her arms as he pulled the T-shirt over her head, and the sight of the pink lacy bra was his undoing. With a groan, he pulled her closer and took those delectable lips with his.

Chapter Twenty-Three

The night spent under a cloudless sky and the myriad of diamond stars had been perfect. The most romantic night Isabella had ever had spent. Forget the five-star hotels and the Michelin-starred restaurants, she'd never forget this night in a campground by the river in the Pilliga Scrub. Sebastian was a skillful lover, and Isabella knew the memory of that night would stay with her for the rest of her life. It didn't rain, but they didn't leave the swag all night.

The next morning, their relationship had taken on a different feel, and it was second nature to stop and hug and kiss as they worked together packing up the campsite.

"Seb?" Isabella waited as he secured the swag on the back of the ute.

"That's me." He turned, and the rush of feeling that slammed into her scared her.

"We're on the same page, aren't we?" she asked.

"Same page?" He reached down and brushed a kiss across her lips.

"We can stay friends after this bit of a fling?"

"Bit of a fling?" His voice was wary, but his eyes were full of…

Damn, they are full of something that I don't want to see.

She nodded. When he smiled it was gone, and she thought maybe she'd imagined that look.

"Of course we can. I'd love to be friends with you. No matter how far away you are."

Since then, she'd been walking on air but at the same time trying to keep in mind that this wasn't going anywhere. She didn't want that, nor did Seb. They were two adults enjoying themselves, but she knew they'd stay in touch. He'd said as much.

On Sunday afternoon, she drove over to Prickle Creek Farm for a visit before she left on Friday, but in hindsight Isabella wished she'd called before she'd driven out on the spur of the moment.

Seb, Liam, and Garth were in the yards working flat chat. Seb had dropped a quick kiss on her lips before he'd gestured to his dirty clothes.

"I'll kiss you properly when we finish," he promised before Liam yelled out for him to send the next beast through the crush.

Helena and Harry were out, Isabella had passed Angie heading to town, and Lucy had been busy cooking in Helena's kitchen. Isabella had only been there five minutes when the phone rang and Lucy answered it.

"Yep, okay." She nodded. "On my way."

Lucy put the phone down and walked over with James in her arms. "Bella, that was Garth. Can you put James in the cot in the spare room for me? I've just got to run this cattle drench over to the guys. I'll only be five minutes. He said as soon as they finish the drenching they'll be back in for a cuppa. Oh, and just keep an eye on those scones I've got in the oven, in case I'm gone a bit longer. They've got about another eleven minutes before they come out."

"Of course." Isabella shook her head as Lucy passed James to her. "You are incredible, you know. Babies, scones, helping out in the paddocks and all the volunteer stuff you do in town. I don't know how you keep up."

"I love it. I'm happy and I never get bored." Lucy looked intently at Isabella. "I have a full life out here...and a man who loves me."

"I'm happy for you. But Luce, don't go getting any ideas. I'm leaving next weekend."

Lucy's mouth turned down. "I know. And you've already told me you and Seb are a holiday romance. Nothing more. But I'm going to miss you, Bella. And Seb will, too."

Isabella held her arms out and a strange feeling ran through her as she looked down at the sleepy little boy when he snuggled into her chest. His plump fist curled into the fabric of her T-shirt, and he yawned before he lifted his head and smiled up at her. Two more cute baby teeth had appeared over the past week. She'd never thought of herself as maternal and didn't plan to settle down and have a family for a long time. There were too many other things to do before she settled into that. But the feel of the warm little body pressed against her chest stirred something unfamiliar inside her.

The door slammed behind Lucy, and Isabella walked around singing softly to James. "Rock-a-bye baby, in the treetop. When the wind blows, the cradle will rock," she crooned softly and was rewarded with another cute smile before James's eyelids fluttered closed. She placed him carefully in the cot and pulled up the light blanket to cover him. She stood there and watched him for a few minutes before she ran a gentle hand over his soft hair and walked thoughtfully back to the kitchen.

The timer clock on the oven buzzed. She picked up an oven mitt and pulled out the tray of scones as Lucy burst back in the back door.

Isabella grinned at her as she hurried over to the kitchen. "I think the only time you sit still is when you're feeding James."

"Did he go down okay?"

"He did."

"That's good. I'm just going to make a batch of pikelets. Liam said they're all starving. They'll be back in half an hour."

Isabella reached down and picked up a mixing bowl. "I'll give you a hand." Since their camping weekend, she'd spent a couple of nights at Prickle Creek Farm and knew her way around the kitchen. She'd been a little bit embarrassed about sharing Seb's room, but Helena had waved a dismissive hand.

"Don't be silly, Bella. Just because we're old doesn't mean we've forgotten what it's like to be in love."

Heat had rushed into her face, and she'd looked down before she caught Sebastian's eye. She had felt his gaze on her, and she knew he wanted her to stay; even though he hadn't said a word, she knew him well enough to read what he was thinking.

Lucy passed her the eggs, and she took the bowl over to the sink. From the kitchen window, Bella could see the three men working together in the yards. She stood and watched as they moved the cattle through from the side paddock into the crush. Sebastian's shoulders were set as he balanced on the rail, pulling the gate across as soon as the beast was in. He was focused on what he was doing. Isabella's mouth dried when he reached up and pulled his T-shirt over his head and threw it over the railing. He leaned forward and his muscles rippled. Those same muscles her fingers had caressed and her lips had kissed. The feeling of loss that slammed into her was physical, and she took a deep breath.

God, I'm going to miss him so much.

An empty feeling settled in her stomach as she cracked the first egg into the bowl. There was no point dwelling on it. She was going, Seb was here to stay, and that was the way it was going to be.

A holiday romance was supposed to be fun and leave you feeling good when it was time to move back to real life. She couldn't stay here. As much as she loved Sebastian, it wasn't an option.

She took another quick breath. Where the heck had that come from? *How can I love him?* It was too fast.

But she knew as clearly as she knew she couldn't stay here that she had fallen in love with him. He was a great guy, and they had so much in common. She understood his commitment to family, and the farm, but she didn't have to agree with it.

It meant she wasn't as important to him as she could have been. But even if she was, she wouldn't consider staying here. It wasn't where she wanted to be, and it wasn't a place where she could develop her career. Okay, so she'd be leaving a bit of her heart behind, but she'd get over it.

Once she was back in familiar territory, she'd be fine.

I will.

"So when do you actually leave, Bella?" Lucy looked at her curiously as she pulled the skillet pan from the cupboard.

"I'm not sure yet. I was going to hire a car, but I don't fancy the drive to Brisbane."

"It is a long way and it's hard to get flights out of Narrabri when you want them."

"Yeah. When I looked, I had to fly from Narrabri to Sydney and then to Brisbane. And it meant an overnight stop in Sydney. Dad offered to drive me to Brisbane." She laughed as she put the eggshells into the bin. "But I said it would be a long round trip for him. Truth is, I don't think I could survive a trip that far in his old beast."

"Um." Lucy cleared her throat. "What about Seb? He's got his new ute."

Isabella shook her head. "No. I won't ask him. Like I said, it's a long way when you have to drive back here."

Besides, Sebastian hadn't offered.

Lucy turned around. "I know!"

"You know what?" With Lucy, you never knew what she was going to come up with.

"Gran and Pop!"

"What? Ask them to drive me?" Isabella shook her head. "No."

"No, silly. You're going on Friday, aren't you?" Lucy turned the pan on and leaned against the benchtop with her arms folded.

"Probably. My London flight leaves early Saturday morning."

"That's perfect. I'll give Gran a call now." She turned to go to the living room, but Isabella held her hand up.

"Whoa right there. What are you organising now?"

"Gran and Pop are leaving for Kakadu this weekend. And I know they're flying out of Brisbane. So I'll find out how they're getting there."

Isabella bit her lip. It made sense. "Okay. That would be good. I'll put the mix in the pan while you call. Where are they?"

"They went into town for lunch with their friends. Ted and Julia are going on the trip with them." Lucy headed for the phone, and Isabella listened as she put the batter into the sizzling butter. As soon as the bubbles appeared she quickly flipped the pikelets over.

"Yes. Sounds good. I'll let her know." Lucy put the phone down and came back into the kitchen. She opened a drawer, took out a clean linen tea towel, and folded it in half, ready for the cooled pikelets to be wrapped.

"So?" Isabella waited.

"It's perfect. They're picking up a coach in Narrabri and taking it to Brisbane on Friday morning. It goes the back way up through Goondiwindi. Gets in about seven on Friday night. Suit you?"

"Sounds perfect. I didn't think of a coach. I'll get online as soon as I get home and book."

And then if Sebastian suggests taking me, I can say no.

• • •

Sebastian pulled out a chair on the verandah and flopped into it. He was hot and sweaty and out of sorts. Wiping the back of his hand over his brow, he grimaced when it came away covered in red dirt. He was sitting here to catch his breath for a moment while Liam and Garth let the cattle out into the paddocks, and then he'd grab a quick shower. He didn't care what Liam wanted. He was taking the afternoon off. He'd been hard at it with bloody cattle all weekend. Liam had insisted on bringing in the herd from the back paddocks on Friday afternoon, and Garth had been free to help them.

Disappointment had made Sebastian gruff. It was Isabella's last weekend here, and he'd really wanted to go camping. Privacy here at Prickle Creek Farm was nonexistent. Isabella had blushed bright red when she'd stayed over this past week; Gran had tapped on the bedroom door with a cup of tea for them both mornings.

And then had sat on the side of the bed and chatted to them!

Honestly. His family!

When he'd told Isabella they couldn't go camping over the weekend, his mood had worsened.

"That's fine," she'd said with a wide smile. "I'll spend it with Dad. It is my last weekend here."

As if I didn't already know that?

He forced the bad mood away and tried to think of a way to address the problem. Finally, he grinned, threw his hat onto the table, and headed for the bathroom. "Get that cuppa going, gals. I'm just having a shower."

He had a plan.

Half an hour later, the scones and pikelets were gone, the teapot had been emptied and refilled twice, and the three couples were sitting on the verandah. Angie had arrived back from town at the same time the men had finished in the yards. Sebastian had his arm around Isabella's shoulders. He had snagged the double swinging hammock chair, and she leaned against him while he played absently with her curls.

"Time we headed home." Garth stood and shook the crumbs off his lap and reached for the last scone. "Thanks for the cuppa."

Liam looked at Angie. "Yeah. I've got some things to do back at the house. We'll see you again before you leave next weekend won't we, Bella?"

"Of course, we all will," Lucy interrupted before Isabella could answer. "I'm going to organise a farewell barbie. Gran and Pop are going away again, and then Bella will be gone. How about Thursday night? Is everyone free? Your dad can come out too, Bella."

Sebastian relaxed when Isabella nodded. "Sounds good. You guys head on home. I'll clean up the kitchen."

"Thanks, Bella. James is due for a feed. We might just get home in time before he cracks it. I'll check Thursday night with Ned and Jemmy. We'll have it at our place. Gran will be too busy packing to worry about having it here at Prickle Creek." Lucy stood and went inside to collect James.

Sebastian stood behind Isabella at the top of the steps as they waved off the two vehicles, his arms linked loosely around her waist. All week he'd been blocking the thought of her leaving and coming up with ways to try to get her to stay. But that wasn't fair to her. She had her career, and this wasn't the right place for her.

Is it the right place for me? Where do I want to be?

Not being able to hold Isabella in his arms, not kiss those beautiful lips, and not wake up beside her—not that they'd had many chances to spend the night together—would be the worst. But at least he would have the memories.

He smiled. Even the one of Gran sitting on the bed with them.

"What are you looking so happy about?" Isabella looked back at him, her soft voice interrupted his thoughts as the cars disappeared around the bend.

"Bed."

She turned in his arms and pushed at this chest. "You have a one-track mind."

Sebastian dropped his forehead to rest on hers. "But isn't it a nice track?"

"It is." She lifted her head, and her lips brushed softly against his mouth. "How long till your grandparents get home?"

Sebastian pulled her closer and then groaned as the sound of a vehicle reached him. "About three minutes."

Isabella giggled. "I feel like a teenager."

He shook his head. "I know Gran wouldn't mind if we went for a 'sleep,' but it's not private enough here for me."

"Oh, so what did you have on mind apart from sleeping?" Her throaty chuckle sent desire rushing though his blood.

"I was going to suggest, seeing we didn't go camping, that we go out and find a nice sunset for some photos, and then I'll take you out for dinner."

"Oh, you romantic! A sunset for photos? Very prosaic." She tipped her head to the side, and he snatched a quick kiss before Gran and Pop drove into the house yard. "Dinner in town?"

"No. In another town."

"Where?" Isabella stepped back from his arms as Pop drove up, but her smile still sent tingles shooting all over him even without her touching him.

"Trust me. It's a surprise." He frowned. "Will your dad mind if you spend the night away?"

"No. He's got his darts grand final on tonight, so I was going to suggest you come into town." Her voice was coy as she looked up at him from beneath her lashes, and Sebastian bit back a groan as her beautiful dark eyes held his. He needed to hold her, but it wasn't the time. He needed to talk to her. He needed to try to convince her to stay with him.

"Okay. You head back to town, and I'll come in about four. Is that okay?"

"Perfect. I've got some things to do online. Now give me a clue. Do I need to get dressed for dinner?"

He burst out laughing and winked at her. "Um, let me think about that."

She shoved him playfully as his grandparents got out of the car. "You know what I mean. Do I need to dress *up* or is it a casual restaurant?"

"I think it would be suitable if you wore that gorgeous creation you wore to the races."

Her face lit up in a smile. "Oh that's good. But I might wear different shoes. I won't be too overdressed for taking photos in the paddocks?"

"Trust me, Bella."

Chapter Twenty-Four

Isabella booked a seat on the coach that was leaving Narrabri for Brisbane on Friday. The more she thought about it, the better the arrangement was. Tonight would be the time to say her private goodbye to Sebastian, and if she shed a tear—and she knew she would—he would be the only one to see it.

It was going to be so, so hard to leave him, but she knew Sebastian had commitments here. Watching the three men work together in the cattle yards today had gone a long way to making her realise that this was his place. He might not be sure of that yet, but he was a decent man, and she knew he would do the right thing.

By his family.

But what about me? a little voice whispered. Was it the right thing to do, letting her leave his life? She forced herself to sit up straight and fight to see sense.

It was a holiday romance. That's what they had both agreed. Now her holiday was almost over and it was time to move on. Just a shame it had taken them so long to get together.

Isabella closed her laptop with a loud snap, and her father looked over at her.

"Okay, *cara*?"

"Yes, all good, Dad. I'm booked on to the coach from Narrabri on Friday morning."

His thick black brows beetled into a frown. "So you are going to leave."

"Of course, I am. You know I was only here for a short visit."

"What about Sebastian?"

"What about him?" Isabella folded her arms and stared at her father as his brow stayed wrinkled.

"I thought—"

"There's nothing to think, Dad. We're good mates and that's it."

This time his eyebrows rose, but his voice remained mournful. "A father can hope."

"And so can a daughter. Did you think any more about going to see Mum?" Turning the tables on him took the pressure off her. She was so close to tears it would only take a few words and she'd lose it.

And she still had five days to get through. And tonight with Sebastian.

"It is a coincidence that you mention it."

"Oh?"

"I was talking to your mother while you were out." The frown was still there, but the voice was lighter. "We have decided that if you persist in this notion of moving to England, we will come and visit you in the summer."

"We?" Isabella watched as a smile tilted her father's mouth.

"Yes, I am going to visit your mother for Christmas. It will be nice to have Christmas in Florence."

Isabella squealed, and he opened his arms for a hug. "Oh,

Dad, I am so happy."

"Don't go getting your hopes up. It's only a visit." His grin was devious. "But she was very happy to hear from me." He held her close. "As long as you are happy, Bella. I am happy."

"There's no need to worry about me, Dad. I'm a big girl now, and I'm really looking forward to going to England and starting my new job. And it'll be even better with you and Mum coming to visit."

"Would you like to come to the club tonight? We could have dinner after my game?"

She shook her head. "One other night this week. Seb's on his way in. He's going to take some photos, and then we're going out for dinner."

"I might see you at the club then after all. Being Sunday night, there's nothing else open," he said.

She caught his eye and smiled. "Sunday night? There's nowhere else to eat any other night, either. Not since the Chinese restaurant closed." Isabella picked up her laptop and headed for the small bedroom. "Anyway, I'm not sure where we're going, but Seb told me to get dressed up."

"That will be nice for you. It might be a long drive to Dubbo, but there are some good restaurants there."

She pushed open the door of her bedroom and put the laptop on the small desk before she crossed to the wardrobe and took out the blue silk dress. She would always remember the Pilliga—and Sebastian—when she touched this dress. Because once she'd worn it out tonight it would be put away. To be pulled out when she was feeling lonely and she would remember the great time she'd had here with Sebastian, and the rest of his family.

It was going to be hard to leave on more than one level. Not only would leaving Sebastian be a huge wrench, but she'd gotten to know Lucy and Jemmy all over again, and meeting Angie had been great, too.

Her first impression of Spring Downs had changed. It wasn't that there was nothing much to do here. Life was what you made it with friends and family. After the first week of being a little bit bored, her time here had been busy and satisfying.

Full of fun and happiness.

And love. Yes, that was the one thing she would have to move away from. Because once she left, she would lose touch with Sebastian. You couldn't have a love affair over Skype.

A holiday romance. And it was coming to an end.

She headed for the shower, trying to come to terms with life without Sebastian.

• • •

Sebastian made a couple of calls after Isabella left and then went into the laundry where Gran was peering into the freezer.

"I was just looking to see what you can have for dinner. Harry and I don't need much more than a piece of toast. We had a baked dinner for lunch, and Julia made us her famous pavlova."

"Got a big favour to ask you, Gran."

She closed the lid of the deep freeze and turned to him. "A favour? What would that be?"

"I'm taking Bella over to Baradine to get some sunset photos for my contract. And then we're staying at a farm a friend of Garth's owns. Problem is, there's no one there and I'll have to take our dinner. I was wondering—"

Before he finished speaking, Gran was reaching for the apron hanging on the back of the door. "So I guess this is a special dinner? A special night? The night when you're going to tell Isabella how you feel about her."

Sebastian narrowed his eyes. "If it is, she'll be the first to hear it, no one else."

"Don't you get stroppy with me, young man."

"Sorry, Gran." He ran his hand over his head, trying to hold back his temper. His grandmother could always get a rise out of him.

"Have you told her yet, you're in love with her? And don't deny it. I've seen the way you look at her. Are you really going to let her go?"

"It's my last chance, isn't it," he said quietly as Gran bustled around the kitchen. He pulled out a chair and sat at the big scrubbed wooden table and a memory of sitting here with his mother and chatting to Gran as she'd cooked many years ago flashed into his mind. Even in those days, Gran had been the one to come to whenever someone had a problem. He'd forgotten about that—or had he blocked it from his mind as he'd tried to deal with his mother's death?

He looked up at her as she stopped beside the table. "I'm sorry, Gran."

"And what would you be sorry for now?" Her voice was brisk as always, but Sebastian knew that she wasn't one to show her feelings. It was very rare to see Gran let go.

"I'm sorry that I didn't say thank you to you. That I never showed you how much I cared about you, Gran."

He widened his eyes as she brushed away a tear with the back of her hand. "Get away with you, Sebastian. You don't have to tell me. I know you do."

Even at the funeral of her three daughters, Gran had been stoic and strong and made sure that the four of them had been okay. She'd looked after Liam and Jemima, and Lucy and him on that dreadful day, and then kept in touch with them as they'd made their way out into the world.

Gran had been the one constant in their lives. And when she'd needed them, they'd all come home.

Eventually.

He owed it to her to stay and help Liam with the farm. It was time to grow up and realise this was where he needed to be. A dark-eyed, dark-haired beauty had taken his focus away for the past few weeks, but he knew where he needed to be.

Tonight he would see if Isabella would stay here with him.

"Would a chicken casserole and some fresh made bread be all right?"

"Perfect. Thank you, Gran."

Gran flicked her fingers onto the leather tie holding his long hair back.

"And when are you going to grow up and get a haircut?"

"I'll think about getting one this week, if you let me pick all the roses in your garden while you cook. And maybe let me filch a bottle of champagne out of Pop's fridge?"

She smiled. "Whatever you think it will take, Sebastian. I love that girl, too. She's the right one for you."

"Um, one more thing." He fiddled with the leather hair tie. Do you still have that sapphire ring of Mum's?"

An hour later, Sebastian had loaded two eskies, his tripod, and cameras into the back of the ute. He'd pulled out his black jeans and his mum's ring was tucked into the pocket of his best black long-sleeved shirt. He smiled. He was feeling like himself again. Seventies music filled the ute as he drove into town, and he was in a fine frame of mind when he parked outside the milk bar. Isabella opened the door with a big smile, and his confidence strengthened.

I can do this.

"Hi there," he said. "Your chariot awaits, *madame*."

"Dad's already gone." She handed him a small bag and closed and locked the door behind her. "Are you going to tell me where we're going?"

"Nope. It's a surprise."

"And all I needed was a toothbrush? I got your text."

"That's all you need." Her nod and smile sent a ripple of pleasure down his spine.

Don't rush. Handle this carefully. He'd practised what he was going to say, and when he was going to say it, all the way into town.

They chatted as he headed through town, past the high school, and then he glanced across at Isabella when he turned onto the Baradine road.

"Baradine?" Her eyebrows lifted. "Isn't that smaller than Spring Downs?"

He nodded. "Best sunsets over there, they tell me."

"So why did you tell me to get dressed up for dinner?"

"We're not going to eat in Baradine. Photos first, then dinner in Bugaldie."

"Bugaldie?" Her brow wrinkled in a frown. "That's even smaller. What are you up to, Sebastian?"

He decided to tell her some of his plans.

But not all.

"A friend of Garth's has a farm stay just north of Bugaldie. It's nestled in a valley west of the main road and it's ours for the night."

"And dinner?"

"Courtesy of Gran." He gestured to the eskies on the back seat.

"Sounds very well organised, but two coolers? You must be hungry," she said with a smile. "How far away? It's not long till sunset."

"Less than half an hour to where I'm stopping to take the photos. Then we'll head to Troy's place." He reached over and held her hand. "And yes, I'm hungry. *Very* hungry."

A short while later, the dirt road to the small lookout

appeared on the right. He turned the ute onto the road and focused on the rough four-wheel drive track ahead. It narrowed and climbed the hill before it levelled out to a large flat area. A couple of kangaroos bounded away, and once they were gone, there was not a living soul to be seen.

He swallowed as he turned the ignition off and practised his words in his head. Isabella opened the door and walked over to the edge of the hill as he unpacked his camera and tripod and one esky. He patted his pocket and was surprised to see his hands shaking.

Great photos these would be if he couldn't stop shaking. He took a deep breath, slung his camera over his shoulder, patted his pocket one more time, and picked up the esky and tripod.

"Oh, Seb. Look at this. How beautiful it is." Isabella twirled and the silk of her dress caught the fading light as the sun hovered above the far horizon. The sky was a brilliant soft blue with shards of gold streaming from the low clouds to the west. The flat plains of western New South Wales stretched as far as they could see in all directions, broken only by the narrow ribbon of road leading north and south.

Not a car or a homestead to be seen. The light was perfect. Bloody perfect. Best he'd seen since he'd arrived.

"Bella?"

She turned and looked at him.

"This wasn't part of my plan, but can I take you in the photo? Those two blues together are amazing." He frowned. "You'd have to sign a disclosure so I could sell them commercially."

"Of course. Just tell me where to stand."

"Wait till I get set up." He knew his voice was clipped, but between his nerves and waiting to get this perfect shot, he felt like someone else. When the creative urge filled him, it was as though he was a different person.

Isabella looked at the esky curiously as he set up his tripod and changed the lens on his camera.

Please don't ask why I took the esky off the ute. He had to get this photo before the light went.

"Okay. You ready?" He lifted the camera and she nodded. "I want you to twirl like you did before. Hold your hands out, lift your chin, and look up at the sky. Let your hair fly in the wind." His voice shook. "You're beautiful."

• • •

Isabella was nervous. She couldn't put her finger on the reason, but there was something in Sebastian's voice, something in his manner, that was different. His usual happy-go-lucky demeanor had been replaced by an intensity that she'd only glimpsed the first night she'd been with him when he'd taken the photos out near the racecourse. His eyes stayed on her every time he lowered the camera, and he'd point to a place for her to move to. She moved and he took hundreds of photographs until the sun slipped behind the horizon in one final flash of brilliant gold. The sky softened to apricot, and the evening stars appeared above.

Sebastian didn't speak as he lowered his camera but held his hand out to her. Isabella took it and walked beside him and waited quietly until he had put the camera and tripod into the ute. When he turned back to her, his eyes were still intense and dark. His voice was low and husky.

"Close your eyes for me, Bella." He put his finger on her lips and smiled. "Don't ask. Just do."

Isabella lifted her shoulders in a shrug, but still the nerves were fluttering in her stomach even more now. She did as she was told. As she stood there with her eyes closed, she could hear Sebastian moving around and a rustle of paper and the sound of the esky being opened. Next minute, his breath brushed her cheek.

"Keep your eyes closed and take my hand."

Again she obeyed, and he led her a few steps. She wrinkled her nose. A strong floral fragrance surrounded her.

"I'll hold you while you sit down." He held her hands as she lowered herself, and she smiled when she realised she was sitting on the esky.

"One more minute. Eyes closed."

She jumped as a cork popped and the next minute the sound of liquid being poured into a glass reached her. She shook her head as her trepidation increased.

She knew him too well and wasn't sure she liked the way this was heading. Unless…unless he'd decided to come with her.

To leave the farm and follow me to England? Maybe? She kept her eyes closed and hoped…and hoped. She fought down the flare of anticipation that was getting stronger every second.

Silence for a moment and then a rustle in front of her, before her hand was picked up in his.

"You can open your eyes now, Bella."

Sebastian was kneeling in front of her. It took a few seconds for her eyes to adjust and she looked around. Roses were strewn on the ground around her, and as she watched, he lifted a glass and passed it to her.

"A real date, Seb?" She smiled. "Roses and champagne, finally?" Her voice trembled with emotion.

Sebastian shook his head. "More than a date." He reached into his shirt pocket and Isabella widened her eyes as certainty flooded through her.

"Bella. I've thought long and hard about this, and I know that time is short." He reached out with his other hand and lifted her chin so that she looked into his eyes. His expression was filled with love and certainty, but she knew his certainty was different to hers. "Maybe if you weren't leaving on Friday, I would have waited but I can't risk losing you. I want you to stay."

She shook her head and bit her lip as her throat ached. Regret sat in her chest like a stone.

No. But then she realised she'd only cried it in her head. She opened her mouth to stop him, but gentle fingers brushed over her lips. "Let me finish."

As he spoke, the tears welled in her eyes and slipped down her cheeks, but he kept talking.

"I love you, Bella. And I know that I want to spend my life with you. I have the perfect solution."

But where? Is he going to say he will come to England with me?

Please.

"I can take on more photographic contracts to supplement the work at the farm, and we can travel around the Outback. There's no need for you to go to England."

All her hopes and dreams sank like a stone.

The tears fell and he lifted his thumb and wiped them away. One cheek, and then the other, and horror filled her when he opened the small black case he held.

The box was dark, and the stone was dark. It was how she felt, as regret became heavier.

"Will you marry me? Make a life together out here?"

Isabella's breath hitched and finally the words came. "No. Seb. Please stop." She jumped up from the cooler, and her flat shoes crushed the roses as she walked away from him, her fist to her mouth, the sweet fragrance making her feel sick. She looked down wordlessly as the glass she had been holding slipped from her fingers and smashed on the ground.

"I can't. This was only a holiday romance. It was never going to be forever." Even as she said the words, she knew she loved him, but she couldn't compromise. If she said yes, and stayed here with him, what would happen to all her hopes and dreams? She couldn't push them aside to stay here, even though the temptation was so strong. After a few weeks—months—maybe, she'd regret it, no matter how much she loved him.

She had come to terms with leaving, and now he had brought all of the emotion surging to the surface again. Shaking her head, she cried out to him.

"Why did you have to do that? Why did you have to ruin everything? I was going to say goodbye to you tonight and make it a night we would both remember. I do"—her breath hitched—"I do care about you…but I can't give up my dreams. If you don't know that, you don't know me."

She stood there shaking as Sebastian got up from the ground and picked up the bottle. He walked over to the edge of the hill and tipped the liquid out, before he came back and opened the esky and put the empty bottle inside. Without a single word, he pulled out some newspaper and crouched down and picked up the broken glass. Then he picked up the esky and put it in the car before he turned to her.

"Get in the car, Isabella." His voice was quiet and flat. "Please. I'll take you home."

The trip back to Spring Downs was silent. The crushed roses beneath her feet as she walked back to the car was a memory that would stay with Isabella for the rest of her life, as was the desolation in Sebastian's eyes as he parked outside the milk bar and waited for her to get out of the car.

"Goodbye, Seb. I'm sorry."

The last thing she saw before she shut the door was the glittering darkness of his eyes.

Chapter Twenty-Five

Gran obviously knew better than to say anything when Sebastian drove in just after nine o'clock that night. He hoisted the esky with the food out of the back seat and took it into the kitchen. Gran and Pop were sitting at the table, a pot of tea between them. He pulled out the ring and handed it to Gran before he went to his room, shut the door, and dropped onto the bed.

So she bloody cared about him, did she? But not enough to give up her dreams. Well, he'd made a right fool of himself, hadn't he? He lay there with his arm over his face, remembering the horrified expression on her face.

Only a holiday romance, she'd said. And more fool him to think he could change it. Of course she didn't want to be out here. Hell, he didn't want to, either.

How could he have had the presumption to think that a simple declaration of love would change her mind? God, what a fool.

A gentle tap at the door interrupted his angry brooding.

"Who is it?" he snapped.

"Gran. Can I come in?"

"If you must." Sebastian knew he was being rude, but he didn't give a rat's—. Gran had seen him worse than this.

She came in and sat down on the end of the bed. "So I'm guessing it was a no?" He'd left the small lamp on beside the bed, and he watched as Gran's fingers lifted the tassels on the bedspread.

"It was an emphatic no."

"Do you want to talk about it?"

"Not really. There's no point."

Her voice was soft and her eyes gentle as she looked at him. "You always were one to rush in, Sebastian. Even when you were the tiniest little boy. Your mother used to say that you would make your mark in the world, and she was right."

He shrugged. "I had to ask her. She's going on Friday."

"I know. And Isabella will be on the same coach as us, and I guess I'll have to sit there and watch her be as miserable as you are."

"Why would she be miserable? "

Gran shook her head. "Because she loves you, sweetheart. She just needs time to realise that the way she feels about you will rise above anywhere you might live or work. Trust me, I know."

A tiny glimmer of hope took root, and then he shook his head. "No, you didn't see the look on her face. She was horrified that I even asked. I feel like such a bloody fool."

He might as well have not spoken as Gran continued. "It is so much like Harry and me. He loved the land, but for me, a girl from the centre of London? Can you imagine what it was like coming out here? There wasn't even a real house. Just the old two-bedroom place his father had built about thirty years before I arrived."

"So your point is?"

His grandmother sighed.

"The point is—the big one that you are missing—is that Harry loved the land. He couldn't leave it to save his soul. If I loved him enough, I had to come here and be with him. And I did, and I came to love it, too."

"So you reckon if I persevered, she'd come to love it, too?"

Gran stood up and wagged her finger at him. "My God, Seb, you are so obtuse. Of course not. Do you know what the difference is?"

He shook his head, but he was beginning to get the point.

"I said Harry loved the land, and he couldn't leave it. Now you tell me why you're here working with Liam?"

"Because it's the family farm?"

"Wrong answer."

"Because you wanted us all to come home and live back here?"

Her voice was sharp. "No, I didn't."

"Oh yes you did. Two years ago."

"I asked you to come back and share that year while your grandfather got back on his feet. It was none of my doing that your three cousins love this land as much as Harry does. That—now listen closely—doesn't mean that *you* have to."

"Hang on." Sebastian focused on something she'd said. "You said the others love it as much as Pop does. What about you?"

"I love Harry," she said simply.

"Oh." The penny dropped, and he got what Gran was saying.

"There's one more thing you need to know," she said. "Your photographic success has not come through luck. You are a brilliant photographer because you work hard at it. You don't have to stay here and prove to us that you have a strong work ethic. We're proud of what you've achieved, Seb."

"Really?"

"Of course we are." Gran looked up at him, and he held his arms out. As she nestled in his arms, Sebastian dropped his chin and rested it on the top of her head. "I love you, Gran."

"And I love you, my boy." Her voice was gruff.

As he walked down the hall a few minutes later, he finally put it together. The very thing that was keeping them apart was what he admired most about Isabella. She knew what she wanted, and she had the courage to go after it.

And that was one of the reasons he loved her.

. . .

On Wednesday morning, Isabella was racking her mind, trying desperately to think of an excuse to get out of the barbeque at Lucy's that night when the phone rang. Trying to come up with a reason had taken her mind off Sebastian. But apart from a broken leg, she couldn't think of a way out of it. At least she hadn't mentioned it to Dad, so she didn't have to tell him they weren't going.

"For you, Bella," Dad hollered. She walked over slowly, looking at the old-fashioned phone as though it would bite her. She took the phone and Dad shook his head as he went back to his newspaper.

"Hello?"

"Hi Bella, It's Lucy. Listen, I'm really cross."

Isabella's throat closed. Of course, she couldn't expect to stay friends with Lucy after she'd rejected her cousin.

Family came first.

"Um, yes? I thought you might be."

"Why? Did Seb ring you first?"

"Ring me?"

"To cancel the barbeque?"

"Um, no." She hadn't talked to Seb since he'd dropped

her off three long days and nights ago. "Did you say cancel?" She clutched at the hope that she wouldn't have to come up with an excuse after all.

"Seb's gone to Sydney with Liam. Gran is busy packing, and Ned and Jemmy have a sports thing on tonight. So we thought that Angie, Jemmy, and I, and Ned and Jemmy's kids would come in and have lunch with you tomorrow in town instead."

"What about school?"

"It's school holidays." Lucy's tone changed. "Didn't you know Seb was in Sydney?"

"No? Why should I?"

Disappointment replaced curiosity. "Oh, I was just hoping—"

"Nothing to be hopeful about there, Luce. I'll see you tomorrow. Do you want to have lunch at the milk bar or the club?"

"How about the milk bar? Give your dad some business."

"Thank you, that's thoughtful of you."

"And Gran said she'll see you on the coach and will say goodbye in Brisbane."

"Okay. Sounds like a plan." Isabella injected some life into her voice. "I'll look forward to it. I'm packing now, so I'll see you tomorrow then."

"Okay, about twelve." Lucy ended the call and Isabella walked thoughtfully into the kitchen. "You've got a crowd coming in for lunch tomorrow, Dad."

Chapter Twenty-Six

Friday arrived faster than Isabella thought it would. Exhausted from not sleeping for three nights, she slept like a log the last night. Lunch on Thursday had been fun, but no matter how much Lucy snooped, Isabella had revealed nothing about Seb's proposal. Saying goodbye was sad, but she extracted a promise from all of them that they would come and visit her in England or Italy, wherever she was, if they travelled.

Dad was quiet as he loaded her two bags into the Citroën. She stood in the doorway of the milk bar and looked around. "Are you sure it's okay to close today?"

"Of course it is. I have to see you off."

They left for Narrabri mid-morning, and Isabella worried the whole way about who would be taking Helena and Harry to the coach stop. At least it took her mind off Dad's driving. As far as she knew, Liam and Sebastian were still in Sydney, and she hoped it would be one of the girls or Ned. It hadn't been mentioned at lunch. She directed her father to the service centre on the outskirts of town where the coach would pick them up.

As they approached the centre, her heart skittered and she could have sworn it missed a beat. Sebastian's ute was parked in one of the spaces near the coach terminal. Her worst fear was realised when she saw him climb out of the car, go around to the back, and lift a suitcase from the rear tray.

"Ah, they beat us." Dad's booming voice made her jump. "Helena said Sebastian was driving when she called me this morning."

"Called you? When did she call you?"

"I think you were in the shower."

"What did she want?" Isabella frowned. She didn't have a clue how to act. Lucy had known nothing about them breaking up. Maybe Seb hadn't told anyone. He was the one she worried about.

"She was just checking you were still getting the same coach."

"Okay."

Her father shot her a curious look as she got out of the car. She picked up her backpack, ran her fingers through her hair, and bit her lips to give them some colour. Holding herself straight once she was out of the car, she sauntered casually over to Sebastian and his grandparents.

"Morning," she said brightly as Dad followed with her bags.

"Hello, Bella." Gran smiled at her and Harry leaned over to kiss her cheek.

Phew, she doesn't know.

Unable to put it off any longer, Isabella lifted her gaze to Sebastian. He was wearing wrap-around sunglasses and she couldn't see his eyes.

Damn him. She pulled hers down from the top of her head and covered her eyes as well.

"Hi, Seb."

"Hello." His voice was husky and a damn tingle ran down her back. Just from his voice, blast it.

"You've been away?" she asked.

"Yes, Liam and I went to Sydney. We got back just in time to bring this pair of travellers to the coach."

Isabella looked around. "Aren't your friends travelling with you?"

"No," Helena said. "They're meeting us in Darwin next week. So we can chat all the way to Brisbane."

Isabella bit back the groan that threatened.

Great.

"That will be nice. You can tell me all about Windsor," she said.

All too soon, the coach came into view, and she turned to hug Dad. She lifted her sunglasses up to kiss him and blinked back the tears as he held her close. "Thanks for having me, Dad. I'll miss you until you and Mum come visit me."

"You take care of yourself, *cara*." He looked at her closely and smiled. "And be happy. In whatever you choose."

Strange words.

"I will, Daddy." One last kiss and she followed the others over to the coach as her father waited by the car.

Sebastian hugged his grandmother, and she was surprised to see him wrap his grandfather in a hug, too. "You two have fun, okay?"

Isabella stood back as Helena and Harry got on the coach. The bus driver took the bags around to the side and stowed them in the big hatch beneath the coach.

"So, this is it." Sebastian walked over and stood close beside her.

"Yep. This is it."

"I'm sorry I put you in that embarrassing situation the other night."

She waved her hand. "All forgotten. I'm sorry I had to

say no."

He stared down at her and she had to fight to hide what she was feeling. She bit her lip and stood straight. But his next words tested her.

"Can I kiss you goodbye?" he asked. "Just to finish off a fun holiday romance?"

She nodded and looked up at Sebastian. He lifted his sunglasses and then reached over and pushed hers back. His eyes were full of emotion, and she blinked quickly, unable to push away the warmth that was flooding through her when he held her gaze for one long minute.

"Goodbye, Bella."

She closed her eyes as he lowered his head and the strong sunlight was blotted out. She opened her mouth and his lips clung to hers as they shared a sweet kiss. His hand cupped the back of her head when they pulled apart, and again they held each other's eyes. Something tugged deep within Isabella, an exquisite emotion that she had never felt before.

"Goodbye, Seb."

She didn't look back as she climbed on the bus and found her seat. Not that she would have seen anything. Her eyes were full of tears.

• • •

Seb broke every road rule he'd ever learned as he jumped in the ute and drove back to Prickle Creek Farm. He should have listened to Gran. If she ever gave him advice again, he'd listen to every word she said. The dear old gal had been right, and he felt like whooping as the ute chewed the kilometres up. If he'd listened to her, he would have had his bag and his camera gear in the ute, but now he had to backtrack. He kept his eye on the clock on the dashboard, but the time seemed to fly by as fast as the kilometres.

Finally, the ute rattled over the grid at the front of Prickle Creek Farm, and he spared a quick smile at the sign at the front. He sent a thank you to whomever was looking after him when he spotted Liam's ute in the hayshed. As Sebastian jumped out of the ute, Liam tipped his Akubra back.

"Where's the fire?"

"Stay there." Sebastian pointed at the car as he ran towards the house. "Don't move. Don't go anywhere."

Liam was still frowning at him when he shoved open the screen door and ran up the hallway. He stuffed as much as he could into his bag and searched frantically for his passport. As long as he had his wallet, his camera gear, and his passport, nothing else mattered. He picked up his tripod and threw it back on the bed. He could buy another one. Liam was still standing beside the ute, scratching his head when he ran back down the steps.

"You've got me beat. Where are you going?" Liam nodded at the gear that Seb was throwing on the back of the ute.

"We're going north. You and me. Now."

"What? North where?"

Sebastian glanced at his watch and did a quick calculation. "I'd say somewhere between Moree and Boggabilla if we don't get a move on."

"What the hell are you on about?" Despite his question, Liam jumped in the ute.

"I'm going after Bella. She loves me." He stated it simply and satisfaction filled him as the words came out. "Gran was right all along. Isabella loves me."

"So she told you this at the bus station?" Liam grabbed for his seat belt as Sebastian fishtailed the ute down the road to the gate. "Slow down if you want to get there in one piece, you hoon."

"No, she didn't. But she does. She kissed me."

"And then when you reach her, are you going to do what I think you are?"

"Yep. I'm going to England."

"Thank goodness for that," Liam said with a grin.

"Why? Won't you miss me?" Sebastian shot a glance at his cousin as they reached the main road.

"Of course I will, but I also know that your heart's not in the farm, and you'll be a damned sight happier taking photos."

"I will." Sebastian cleared his throat. "Ah. Just checking. Are you happy to come with me and bring the ute back?"

"I guess I'm here now."

Just under an hour later as they drove through Moree, Sebastian pulled the car to a quick stop outside the local IGA.

"What now?" Liam shook his head. "Did you forget something?"

Sebastian grinned at Liam and ran inside.

When he came back, Liam shook his head as Sebastian carefully placed six bunches of red roses on the back seat.

"You've totally lost it, Seb. You know that? You're off your flaming rocker."

"And happy as a pig in mud. Or I will be soon."

"I just hope you're right," Liam muttered as Sebastian accelerated down the road. "And watch out. There's a speed camera north of town."

Sebastian slowed the ute for the first five kilometers out of town and then planted it again. According to Gran, the coach would have stopped at Moree for a half-hour rest stop so it shouldn't be far ahead of them now.

"You're going to get us arrested at this speed." Liam's words held a note of warning, and Sebastian eased back on the accelerator as they crested a hill.

"You bloody beauty!"

The coach was only a couple of hundred metres ahead of

them. He floored it again and Liam shook his head.

• • •

Isabella was thankful that Helena and Harry were sitting a couple of rows ahead of her, and the seat beside her was empty. The elderly man across the aisle from her had gone straight to sleep and hadn't even woken when they'd stopped for their first rest break at Moree.

So she could shed as many tears as she liked without anyone looking at her. She wiped her eyes with her sodden tissue and pulled her sunglasses down when she noticed Helena walking up the aisle to sit with her. Every time she stopped crying, the thought of never seeing Sebastian again would make the tears start afresh.

What have I done?

She shook herself and tried to push the emotion away. Once she was on the plane and making her way to England, this feeling would ease. It would be in the past. In future years, she'd look back at the holiday fling and her first proposal as a fond memory and be able to smile about it. Her lips trembled, and she hitched a shaky breath.

I'm not the right one for Sebastian. He needs a country girl. Someone who'll settle on the farm with him. Someone who's happy to stay in the Outback.

Determination filled Isabella. No matter how much she loved him, she couldn't do that. She couldn't. No matter how much that hurt, she couldn't imagine spending the rest of her life in the bush. So it just went to show that she didn't love him enough, so they *weren't* right for each other.

She just had to figure out how to get on with life without Sebastian in it.

And then she sat up straight and opened her eyes. They *were* right for each other. She loved him, and she knew he loved her. For God's sake, he'd proposed and she'd rejected him.

His grandmother eased into the seat beside her and snapped on the seat belt. "Harry's gone to sleep." She looked closely at Isabella. "I just wanted to make sure you were all right."

Isabella nodded and stuffed the wet tissue into her pocket. "I'm fine." She cleared her throat.

"You don't look fine." Helena's voice was brisk as she passed a clean tissue across the seat. She wasn't one for holding back. "I think you love my boy, don't you?"

Isabella nodded mutely. "I do."

"So what are you going to do about it?"

Tears welled in her eyes again. "Figuring out how to stop crying would be a good start."

Helena patted her arm. "The tears will dry up. I cried buckets of tears when I left Harry all those years ago. When he came back to Australia."

"That's good." Isabella sniffed and wiped her nose. "To know they'll stop, I mean."

"I want you to know something, and it might give you some hope. I know that boy well—and trust me, I know what makes him tick. Much more than he realises."

Isabella looked up curiously. "And…"

"And I know he loves you. Don't you worry; he won't let you go."

Isabella shook her head. "He's got commitments here. He shouldn't leave." She looked up at Helena. "You all want him to stay here. It's me that's the sticking point. But I've made up my mind. I can't let him go."

"We all want Sebastian to be happy. It doesn't matter where he is. And as I said to Harry before, if we're totally honest, we all knew that his heart wasn't in the farm." She took Isabella's hand in hers. "But sweetheart, it shows you the measure of the man he is. He knew we wanted him to have a go at it, and he came out and he gave it his best shot. And if you hadn't come along, he probably would have kidded himself he was happy here."

Isabella shook her head. "At the next stop I'm getting off. I'm going back to ask him to come with me."

"I don't think you will need to, if I know my boy." Helena's smile was sweet.

A glimmer of hope kindled in Isabella's chest. "Really?" she whispered. "You think if I called him and told him I love him, there's a chance for us?"

Helena looked out the window of the bus and then turned back to Isabella with a smile. "Sweetie, I don't think you're even going to have to call."

Isabella frowned as the bus drew slowly to a stop beside a park on the side of the narrow country highway.

"Good. I'm going to get off now," she said.

The coach driver picked up the microphone, and there was laughter in his voice. "Just an unexpected delay folks. We're ahead of time so it's nothing to worry about. If you'd like to get out and stretch your legs, it's another hour before our next stop."

"Come on. Let's stretch our legs and get some fresh air." Helena had the strangest smile on her face. "I guarantee you will feel much better."

"If I get off, I'm staying off." Isabella unclipped her seat belt and followed Helena and most of the passengers to the door of the bus. Helena tapped Harry's shoulder on the way out.

"Harry. Come on. You need to get off the bus. Now. Quick."

"Wha—?" He came awake with a snort and was on his feet and following them, still rubbing his eyes.

Isabella pulled her sunglasses down as she stepped onto

the grass verge at the side of the road. The other passengers had walked across to the small park where there were a couple of tables with a roof overhead to provide shade.

As she turned around she blinked, and the deep breath she was about to take turned into a gasp.

A white ute was parked half across the road, blocking the bus from going any farther. Liam was leaning against the passenger door, his arms folded.

But it was the man walking towards her who sent her heart skyrocketing. Her mouth dropped open, and she lifted her hands to her lips as Sebastian dropped to one knee in front of her—and the forty coach passengers.

A giggle rose in her chest; she could barely see him for the dozens of red roses that filled his arms.

"Hello, Sebastian." Her voice was even as she managed to greet him as though kneeling on a deserted Outback road, holding dozens of roses against his chest, was just a normal occurrence.

"Hello, Bella."

She leaned over and put her hand on his shoulder and was surrounded by the sweet fragrance of the ruby blooms. "A bit of a coincidence to see you out here." Her voice was wary because no matter what Helena had said, Isabella wasn't sure how he'd answer her question.

"No coincidence about it."

"How did you get the coach driver to stop?"

"I got him on the radio."

"Why?" she asked as she looked down at him.

"This is where I have to be."

"Where's that, Seb?" Her voice was soft as his eyes held hers.

"Wherever you are, Bella. I want to share your dreams."

Her breath hitched again, and she reached out and touched his face. "*My* dreams?"

"Yes. And I know now that our dreams aren't here. Not now, maybe one day. Maybe. Maybe not." He pushed himself to his feet and looked down at the roses with a grin. "I want to put my arms around you when I tell you how much I love you, but I can't."

"Put them on the road, Seb." The little glimmer of hope in her chest had blossomed like the roses. Strong, colourful, and all pervading, it had blossomed into trust and certainty that this was the right thing for them.

Before he could put the roses down, Helena and Harry reached for them. "Give them to us, Sebastian," Helena said with a smile.

He handed over the roses and put his arms around Isabella. She turned her face into the warmth of his neck as he lowered his head to rest it against hers.

"Bella, is it okay if I come to England with you?"

Her head flew up and she stared at him, her eyes wide as surprise slammed into her.

"So that's a yes or a no? Talk to me, Bella."

She lifted her arms around his neck and held him tight. "I was going to get off the bus and come back. I was going to beg you to come with me."

"No begging required, sweetheart. Did you really think I'd let you go? I'm coming with you."

"You're coming with me? Now?" Isabella laced her fingers behind his neck, not game to let him go. "On the coach?" She frowned, unable to process what he was saying. "To Brisbane?"

"Yes. To wherever you're going. The farm's not the right place for me. Gran helped me see that." He lifted her hand to his lips and kissed it. "Maybe England's not where we'll end up, but we'll give it a try. Maybe Florence? Maybe Rome? Maybe…who knows? It doesn't matter, Bella, as long as we're together, we'll be happy."

As Isabella looked up at Sebastian, her heart swelled with love for this man.

My man.

"And yes, I have a coach ticket. That's why I brought Liam. He's going to take the ute back. I'm all packed. All I need is you…and my camera. And there's a spare seat next to you, I believe."

Isabella lifted her arms around his neck and pulled Sebastian's head closer to hers.

"Kiss me." She pressed her lips against his mouth. "Kiss me. Please, kiss me." Warm lips moved against hers, and she remembered the moment he had first saved her. "Kiss me as if you can't bear to let me go."

An unbelievable feeling ran through her as his hold tightened and she closed her eyes. His lips claimed hers, and a cheer rose from the coach passengers surrounding them. Isabella opened her eyes as he murmured against her lips.

"I'm kissing you because I *won't* let you go, Bella. I'll follow you wherever you take me."

Epilogue

Twelve months later

Isabella stood on the edge of the manicured green lawn outside The Three Ducks restaurant in the village of Maplethorpe in England. She looked up at the pale eggshell-blue sky. It was nothing like the big sky of Outback Australia. That sky would always be very special to her, just like a night that had threatened rain and she'd slept inside a swag.

The night I fell in love.

She smiled as she smoothed down the white silk of her wedding dress. Inside the restaurant, her love was waiting for her. Waiting for her to come in and commit her life to him.

"Ready, Bella?" Her mother's voice intruded on her happy thoughts.

Isabella looked up, and her eyes pricked with tears as she looked at her old and new family. "I'm ready, Mum."

"Oh no, you don't." Jemima pulled out a tissue, reached across, and dabbed lightly at Isabella's eyes. "I didn't do your makeup for you to cry and have it run before you even get married."

Isabella blinked them away. "They're happy tears."

Lucy smiled. "Let her cry, Jemmy. You cried bucket loads of tears on your wedding day."

"I did." Jemima nodded.

"You look beautiful, Bella, tears and all." Angie's voice was soft and Bella reached out and squeezed her hand, although it was hard to get past Angie's pregnant stomach.

Isabella looked at her bridal party and couldn't help the huge smile that lifted her lips. Her father was waiting by the door and was going to walk her in with Mum. As she watched, Dad put his arm around her mother and dropped a kiss on her cheek. Happiness for her parents completed her. The past twelve months had been wonderful. Her job at The Three Ducks was everything she'd dreamed, Sebastian had picked up a contract with a top London magazine, and now everyone who was important in their lives had come to England to be a part of their wedding day.

Lucy, Jemima, and Angie were her three matrons of honour, dressed in pale blue. Kelsey and Gwennie were bridesmaids in white lace. Ryan and Lucy and Garth's little James were ring bearers. Jemima carried Charlie, their almost-one-year-old son. Isabella had said it wasn't fair that he miss out. Lucy and Garth's new little girl, Charlotte, was asleep in the pram.

Inside, the rest of the family were waiting. Gran and Pop hovered near the door, ready for the bridal party to come in. Liam was Seb's best man, and Garth and Ned were the groomsmen.

As Isabella waited, the strains of their chosen song drifted out on the air, and her mother and father walked over and stood on each side of her.

"Are you ready, *cara*?" Dad asked with a smile.

"Yes, I am," she said.

. . .

Sebastian stood at the front of the restaurant. A small formal area had been set aside for the ceremony. He glanced down at his watch and Liam laughed.

"Seb, it's approximately thirty seconds since you last checked the time. It's not going to go any faster. If you hadn't insisted on getting here early, you wouldn't have had to wait so long for the girls to arrive."

They both looked up as Gran hurried across the restaurant. "Okay, they're ready." She nodded to the young man manning the sound system, and he switched on the music.

Calm flooded through Sebastian as the strains of "Only When You're Sleeping" drifted through the room. He looked up as Isabella walked towards him, and love flooded through him.

He took her hand and they stepped up to the celebrant. Lucy came over behind them and lifted Bella's veil. Bella's gaze held Sebastian's, her beautiful rosy lips tilted in a smile. He looked down at her and was moved by the expression of sheer joy and love on her face.

He mouthed to her, *You are beautiful*, as the strains of the music faded and the ceremony began.

A cheer went up as the celebrant pronounced them man and wife, and Seb looked down at Bella as her fingers tugged on the sleeve of his dress shirt.

"Seb?" Her voice was soft.

"Yes, sweetheart?"

"Kiss me." She pressed her lips against his mouth. "Kiss me, quick. Please, kiss me." Soft, warm lips moved against his. "Kiss me, as if you can't bear to let me go."

"I'll never let you go." He lowered his lips to hers and smiled as she sighed.

A satisfied sigh.

A breeze light as a baby's breath and as warm as a kiss teased curls from the flowers in her hair. The children let go of their parents' tight hands and ran around laughing, sensing the happiness in the room.

Helena clutched her hat and held on to Harry with her other hand.

"All is well with our family, Harry," she said.

He smiled down at her. "It is, Helena. We've come full circle." He reached over and kissed her cheek. "You know, you don't look any different from that girl from Notting Hill I fell in love with all those years ago."

"Get away with you, you silly old man," Helena said, but her smile was wide and her eyes filled with happiness. The family they had made was around them, and love was in the air.

Acknowledgments

As always, thank you to my awesome editor, Erin Molta. I love working with you!

And a special thank you to my critique partner, Susanne Bellamy. A fabulous author and a true friend!

About the Author

Annie Seaton lives on the edge of the South Pacific Ocean on the east coast of Australia with her own hero of many years. Their two children are now grown up and married, and three beautiful grandchildren have arrived. Now they share their home with Toby, the naughtiest dog in the universe, and Barney, the rag doll kitten. When she is not writing, Annie can be found in her garden or walking on the beach…or most likely on her deck overlooking the ocean, camera in hand as the sun sets. Each winter, Annie and her husband leave the beach to roam the remote areas of Australia for story ideas and research. Readers can contact Annie through her website annieseaton.net or find her on Facebook, Twitter, and Instagram.

Find your Bliss with these great releases...

No Cowboy Required
a *Biggest Little Love Story* by JoAnn Sky

Grace Harper is a pro at handling the unexpected—which comes in handy when she inherits the ranch she ran away from years ago...along with a young, autistic stepbrother she's never met. And because nothing ever goes easy for her, Grace finds her frustrating, sexy ex-flame, Noah, taking care of JJ. But if she's getting out of this nowhere town, she'll have to find a way to keep from throttling Noah—without kissing him first.

Back in the Rancher's Arms
a *Trinity River* novel by Elsie Davis

Part of loving the girl next door meant making sure she followed her dreams. Dylan just never expected it to take this long for Kayla to come home. Though Kayla doesn't want to face Dylan again, she can't say no to being maid of honor at her cousin's wedding. But Dylan already lost the woman he loved once. This time, he's determined to win her back...

The Cowboy's Homecoming Surprise
a *Fly Creek* novel by Jennifer Hoopes

Single mom Peyton Brooks's first Friday night out—with adults—in forever isn't exactly going the way she'd expected. She can line dance at the local dive bar with the best of 'em, but she can't shake the feeling she's completely out of her depth. Then the first man she ever loved walks in the door, bringing chaos, especially since the handsome cowboy's the father of her daughter. This definitely calls for whiskey...

The Bookworm and the Beast
a novel by Charlee James

Shy, bookish Izzy is happy to accept a job as a temporary assistant, until the grumpy author claims he didn't actually hire her. He might be as handsome as a storybook prince, but his prickly personality and resistance to all things Christmas are sure to make for a chilly holiday season. Derek soon realizes Izzy could be the perfect solution to his interfering family this Christmas...if she'll agree to pretend to be his live-in girlfriend.

Made in the USA
Columbia, SC
12 February 2022